Nidhi Arora ha
and now Lond
inhabit the wor..
been featured in journals and anthologies including *Best New Singaporean Short Stories*, *Quarterly Literary Review Singapore*, *Out of Print*, *Sonder*, *The Aleph Review*, *The Hooghly Review*, *Cha: An Asian Literary Journal*, *Litro*, *Pluto* and *Tinkle*. *The Lights of Shantinagar* is her first novel.

The Lights of Shantinagar

Nidhi Arora

unbound

First published in 2025

Unbound
An imprint of Boundless Publishing Group
c/o Ketton Suite The King Centre, Main Road,
Oakham, Rutland, England, LE15 7WD
www.unbound.com
All rights reserved

© Nidhi Arora, 2025

The right of Nidhi Arora to be identified as the author of this work has been asserted in accordance with Section 77 of the Copyright, Designs and Patents Act, 1988. No part of this publication may be copied, reproduced, stored in a retrieval system, or transmitted, in any form or by any means without the prior permission of the publisher, nor be otherwise circulated in any form of binding or cover other than that in which it is published and without a similar condition being imposed on the subsequent purchaser.

Text design by Jouve (UK), Milton Keynes

A CIP record for this book is available from the British Library

ISBN 978-1-78965-199-7 (paperback)
ISBN 978-1-78965-202-4 (ebook)

Printed in Great Britain by Clays Ltd, Elcograf S.p.A.

1 3 5 7 9 8 6 4 2

MIX
Paper | Supporting responsible forestry
FSC® C018072

To Shireesh, Rish and Sifat – my lights

House no. 1

Mr and Mrs Kapoor
- Om and Mahima
  - Luv
  - Kush
- Dev and Sumi*
- Vivek

✺

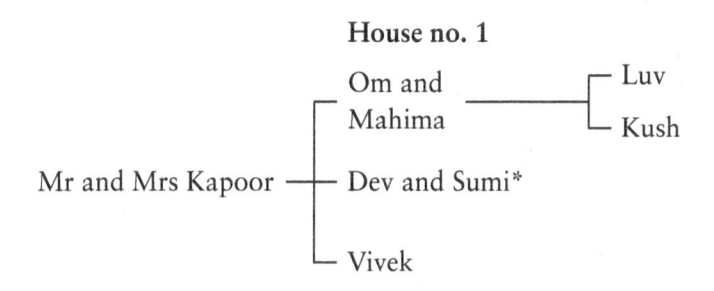

House no. 2

Mr and Mrs Bansal — Dhruv

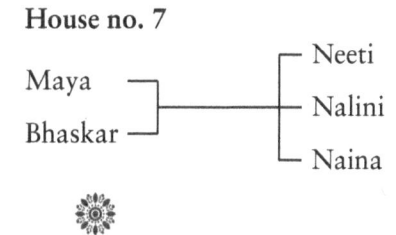

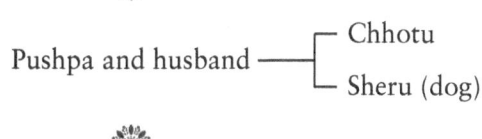

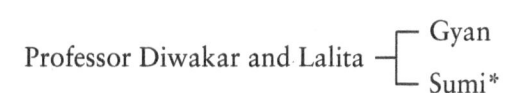

✺

House no. 7

Maya / Bhaskar
- Neeti
- Nalini
- Naina

✺

Pushpa and husband
- Chhotu
- Sheru (dog)

✺

Professor Diwakar and Lalita
- Gyan
- Sumi*

The Things We See, Part I

It was a well-known fact in all of Shantinagar that the only chai Mrs Kapoor liked was the one she made herself, especially the first cup in the morning. She was pernickety about how long the water boiled before adding tea granules, when and how much milk to add, and the one-and-three-quarters spoons of sugar, so that she could tell herself that she did not take two. She let it simmer till it acquired the exact shade of muddy brown she liked.

"The colour of the holy Ganga gurgling down the hills of Rishikesh," she'd say. "In fact, when I die, don't bother getting gangajal, just put a few drops of chai in my mouth," she was fond of saying to her family.

"Never do such a thing," Mr Kapoor would say with a serious face, wagging his forefinger. "What if she comes back to life for more?!"

And everyone would laugh.

Mahima, the elder daughter-in-law, had perfected the art of making chai the materfamilia's way the day she entered the house six years ago. She watched closely when Mrs Kapoor made the morning round and reproduced the exact same concoction in the afternoon. Mrs Kapoor took one tentative sip, not used to liking tea made by anyone other than herself. What she tasted was absolute submission and a fervent desire to please, in return for being admitted into the inner circles of the family. In the next few months, Mrs Kapoor handed over the morning chai-making to her, followed by other household responsibilities like managing Pushpa, their helper of many years, and even the finances.

So when the second son, Dev, married Sumi and brought her home, Sumi found that she had two masters to please. And as is usually the case, the gatekeeper was far more ferocious than the real master. Sumi's kitchen debut was chai too. She made it in the afternoon, when everyone was rousing from their naps. She flavoured it with elaichi, filling the kitchen with the fresh and festive aroma of cardamom. Mrs Kapoor tasted it with the cautiousness of one marking a final term paper. Mahima watched her for a reaction like a student waiting for results. The chai was a shade stronger than Mrs Kapoor liked and sweeter than she permitted herself. It was not a bad cup of tea by any measure. In fact, before she could say anything one way or another, Mr Kapoor smacked his tongue and let out a loud, appreciative sigh. Sumi breathed a little easy, but not fully, as the main verdict was yet to come. One more time, Mrs Kapoor was cut short, this time by the senior daughter-in-law.

"Mummyji doesn't like any flavouring in her chai," Mahima said. "She likes it plain and simple."

"She likes Rishikesh. You've added things and made it the Ganga of Haridwar," Mr Kapoor said. "I say, Ganga is Ganga and tea is tea. Very nice, beta."

"It's not like that," Mrs Kapoor clarified. "This is different, that's all. I don't mind it in the afternoon, but let Mahima continue making the morning one." Mahima gloated at retaining the prime spot.

Sumi did not mind one way or another. Her mother had found a maths teaching position for her at the local secondary school, here in Shantinagar. With her Master of Science, Sumi was overqualified and welcomed humbly by the school. It gave her the time she needed to polish her application for a doctorate in quantum physics. Until then, she left home at quarter past eight in the morning and spent the day surrounded by numbers and books. She returned by three, which still gave her an hour to get fresh, read the newspaper and get tea ready for when everyone woke up from their siestas.

Afternoons in the house followed a ritual. Post lunch, Mrs and Mr Kapoor took a nap in the living room. Comprising a dining area and a lounge with a colour CRT television, it was quite literally the living room: it was the room where they ate, prayed and slept. Adjacent to the television was a large mandir in an alcove and a glass showcase that covered most of the wall. There was a divan stacked under the showcase, generous for one person but not enough for two.

The opposite wall opened into a veranda. Its window was fitted with a cooler. Pushpa filled the cooler with water twice a day. It was switched on after lunch. Not before, for the food would get cold. Once they had cleared lunch at about two in the afternoon, they rolled out a mattress on the floor. Mrs Kapoor claimed the divan and Mr Kapoor lay on the floor. He said it made his back feel better. They slept till about four, in the dark, cooled hall, while Mahima retired to her own room and Pushpa did the laundry in the veranda.

At around four, Sumi prepared five cups of tea. She kept Pushpa's tea in her designated cup in the kitchen and took four cups to the living room. Mrs Kapoor liked to drink her afternoon tea without drawing the curtains, in the darkened room, in full blast of the cool air on her face while the hot liquid trickled down her throat and went straight to her soul. Everyone else joined her quietly, with only the sound of the cooler and Pushpa's washing coming from the veranda. After they finished, Mrs Kapoor would take the cups to the kitchen and Mr Kapoor would draw the curtain and allow the day to resume.

One afternoon, however, the peace was broken. Just after they had finished their tea, Mahima went to the kitchen and created a row that could be heard all the way to the last house in the lane. The prayer plate was missing. It was no ordinary plate. Made of silver, with a dancing peacock engraved on it, it had come with the many things Mahima had brought from her parents' home in her trousseau. But more than anything else, it was the plate that Sumi, the new bride, had taken out of the prayer room, and placed near the sink in the kitchen, next to all the unclean utensils, to be washed.

The mandir was large enough to fit one person. The walls were lined with pictures of Hindu gods and goddesses. The centrepiece was an idol of Mata Rani, the Mother Goddess, decked out in red like a bride, riding a tiger, her black tresses flowing, holding weapons, flowers and blessings in her eight hands. There was an unspoken routine for the mandir based on everyone's morning departure from the house. The first one to say his prayers and light the diya, the earthen lamp, before leaving the house was Dev. Next in line were Luv and Kush, Om and Mahima's five-year-old twins, even if all they could manage was to brush the floor with their hands and touch their foreheads before making a dash for their school bus. Mrs and Mr Kapoor took their turns in quick succession before their eldest son, Om, sought blessings before he left for work. Mahima chose to be the last, out of a sense of responsibility to the mandir. When Sumi joined the family, Mahima offered her the slot just before her own.

Now, Sumi had been brought up on a healthy dose of atheism. Her parents did not go about announcing it, for that ruffled too many feathers. They joined the rituals and festivals around them, but in their home, they preferred to read scriptures and debate on morality. Sumi realised that this was her turn to do the same. Not accepting her slot would be unnecessarily disruptive, so she accepted it quietly. There was only one problem. She did not know many prayers other than the gayatri mantra, which had found its way into her head just by being around rituals and, for the first time in her life, she was grateful for it. Neither was she familiar with the protocol of touching things with the right hand or circling her head with the holy smoke of the diya. To obfuscate things further, she was left-handed, and therefore clumsy with her right hand, especially when it came to nimble tasks like lighting a matchstick or dipping the ring finger in the vermilion powder and touching it to the centre of her forehead. So instead of faking prayer, she did what she did best. She used her ten minutes in the mandir to tidy up. Pushpa was not allowed in the mandir. As a result, it hardly ever got a good cleaning. Sumi started by dusting all the pictures and idols. A baby lizard scuttled from under Lord Krishna's picture and made a dash for his predecessor, Lord Ram. Another day she moved on to the ceiling and cleaned the cobwebs. And so it happened that one day, she spotted the plate that held the diyas and incense sticks. It was caked with sticky black gunk of years of oil-drippings and ash-droppings. She took the silver plate to the kitchen for washing. That was the last anyone saw of it.

Mahima was livid at the disappearance and took it as a personal offence. Her rant lasted the entire afternoon. It was hard to say what angered her more. Was it that the plate was a gift from her parents to this house, or that Sumi had deemed it in such dire need of cleaning, or that something had vanished under her watch? Everyone joined the search for the plate. Mrs Kapoor mumbled platitudes like "where can it go, I'm sure it is here somewhere." Mahima went through the kitchen, turning over every plate and bowl, pan and saucepan there was. She wouldn't let the matter go. She was angry with Sumi, but she took it out on Pushpa.

"You were the last person to have seen it."

"Yes, but I did not touch it. I know you don't like me to touch it."

"Then where did it disappear?"

"Why are you looking at me?" She glared at Mahima. Her presence in the family predated Mahima's. She did not consider herself a servant. When anyone in the house could not remember where they had kept a set of keys or a sock or even a piece of paper, they waited for Pushpa to turn up the next morning and point them to it. For all practical purposes, she was a member of the household. She did not take the insinuation lightly.

Mahima glared back and walked off into the living room. She looked under the sofas and beds, in the store and all the cupboards. Sumi and Mrs Kapoor followed her lead and looked into every nook and cranny. Sumi went through the showcase. She looked behind the black-and-white picture of the three brothers Om, Dev and Vivek in buttoned-up shirts and shorts. Vivek, the youngest of the brothers, who was away at college, was a smaller version of Dev. Sumi tipped the coloured picture of Luv and Kush and gave both frames a quick swipe with her finger as she placed them back. She went through the crockery collection plate by plate, making a mental note to wash the whole lot when the time was right. She did not touch the toy Pomeranian whose fur, once snowy white, had turned to a mix of grey and brown over the years. The pair of wooden dolls wobbled their heads sideways, saying the plate wasn't there. Then they swivelled their hips as if to say, "not here either". In the centre of the showcase stood an ivory elephant of medium size, studded with bright red and green stones. The stones were not precious, and some of them were coming loose. The elephant looked tired. Sumi felt its legs, hoping they might bend and she might sit it down. She whispered to the elephant to please step this way so she could wipe the shelf. She promised to put a cushion under it later. So engrossed was she in this one-sided conversation that she forgot she had company. She found Mrs Kapoor looking at her, like a teacher looks at her favourite student doodling in maths class. The teacher nodded in the direction of the lounge and they both agreed, silently, to move the search party there. They found pencils, batteries, combs, earrings and many other things that had been lost and forgotten, but that only added to Mahima's frustration.

"Look for a silver plate and find chewed up pencils," she grumbled.

"Don't worry, beta. It has gone from The Mother's abode. She will give it back ten times over," Mrs Kapoor said.

"The house is getting a thorough cleaning too!" Sumi couldn't help saying.

The Things We See, Part I

"We better be careful, otherwise the whole house will get cleaned," Mahima snapped.

All this commotion was too much for Mr Kapoor to handle. He changed into shirt and trousers and stepped out of the house on the pretext of getting milk.

Usually, when Mr Kapoor ventured out in the late afternoon, he returned with samosas. He brought exactly ten, one for each person, including Om and Dev who did not return until dinner and even one for Vivek, his youngest son, who was miles away at college, as well as one for Pushpa, in case she was still around.

Everyone devoured them except Sumi. Mr Kapoor's favourite samosa wallah operated out of a little garage at the far end of their local market.

"Have you seen his hands, Daddyji?" Sumi said.

"Why will I see his hands, beta? I go there for his samosas. They are hot; come on, eat."

"His fingernails are black," she said, scrunching her nose with disgust.

"That is why I don't look. If you look at things too closely, you'll find something you don't like. Come, eat while it is still hot."

Sumi smiled, shook her head politely to the proffered samosa. He and Mahima shared hers and the extra one for Vivek.

Mr Kapoor let out a loud appreciative belch as he wiped his oily lips.

Daughters and Sons

Word of the missing plate spread quickly, and later that evening, Maya and Mrs Bansal came over for chai.

Unlike the matchbox-like, three-storeyed faculty building of Sumi's parents' house, houses in Shantinagar took their space. They were laid out in rows separated by narrow alleys, with their backs to each other. The Kapoor house was the first in the lane. Their next-door neighbours, at number two, were the Bansals, owners of the local grocery store. Right behind the Kapoor house was number seven, which belonged to Maya. Sometimes Sumi would be staring outside the kitchen window lost in thought and find herself looking straight into Maya's kitchen.

Mahima, Maya and Mrs Bansal were like sisters. They spoke to one another on the phone every day around noon, with such punctuality that Mr Kapoor claimed to set his watch to when the phone rang. They took turns meeting at one of their homes every week, to confabulate on any matter that may have slipped through calls.

Mrs Bansal had fair skin and every passing year

deposited a layer of prosperity around her middle. Her hair was knotted in a careless bun and she smelled of soap. Not of any particular soap, but the clean smell of soap in general, of all the soaps they had in their store, the extra stock of which was stored in their home.

Mahima said that the Bansals moved to Shantinagar when Dhruv was a year old. They had had their eyes set on the neighbourhood for a few years, and when they had enough savings, they bought house number two. Shantinagar was the right place for them, where people had enough, but not too much. Just like them. They started with a small shop that sold different types of flour that Mrs Bansal ground herself and were now proud owners of the largest grocery shop in the area.

Although they saw each other practically every other day, they still invited the Kapoors over for dinner to welcome the new bride. When she entered their house, the first thing Sumi noticed was the smell. Their house smelled like their shop. It was a mix of whole wheat, rice, gunny bags and detergents. They used one of their bedrooms as an additional store for their inventory. When Mahima or Maya or any other neighbours needed something late at night or early in the morning, Mrs Bansal took it out of the store and sent Dhruv to deliver it. She recorded these transactions in a register. Payments could be made in cash or kind, upon delivery or later. It was a parallel economy that ran on goodwill.

Maya's house, on the other hand, was tastefully decorated with artisan furniture, not expensive but beautiful.

Like Maya herself. She had large eyes set off with thick lashes and long, jet-black hair that reached below her waist. Her saris were always starched, crisply ironed and tightly draped, she wore matching lipsticks and bindis and single-handedly ran a tiffin business.

Maya was the youngest of them all but, according to Mahima, she had gone through a great deal in life, so if experience was any measure of seniority, she outdid most people in the neighbourhood. The very same people who placed food orders with her a week in advance said all kinds of things about her as they licked her kadhai gosht off their fingers. It was rumoured that her oldest daughter, Neeti, was born out of wedlock. It tied in well with the rest of the story that her husband, Bhaskar, disappeared leaving her in charge of three young daughters. But Mahima was not one to dwell on these scandals about her friend. People said anything, especially if it was about a woman who was good-looking and independent. She had known Maya's husband briefly. Sure, Bhaskar was a widower and quite a bit older than Maya, but Mahima had known him to be a simple man, always in his white kurta pyjama and chappals. He was a helpful neighbour, a loyal husband and a devoted father, his only vice being cigarettes, but those too he smoked where people didn't mind and never in the presence of elders. On Sundays, he took his daughters cycling to the river. One Sunday, about six years ago, he was seen without his bicycle, walking in the same chappals, never to return. Mahima did not press Maya for details; she respected her friend's privacy. But for the rest of Shantinagar, it was a major incident in their sleepy colony where nothing of much importance ever happened.

Shantinagar, as the name suggested, was a quiet locality where ordinary people went about their ordinary lives, earning livelihoods, sending children first to school, then to engineering or medical college, looking after ageing parents, reading the newspaper, watching cricket, praying to their gods, arguing over which mango had more flavour – langda or daseri – and which politician was more corrupt. Each day was more or less like the previous one, and when it was done, people checked in on their neighbours to make sure that their day had been no less ordinary.

This trio was no different. When they met, they resumed their on-going conversation about their children. Their children went to the same school. Textbooks had been passed back and forth from one family to another so many times over the years, and bore notes in so many handwritings, that there was no telling who they had originally belonged to. Luv and Kush were only five, but Mahima spoke of her youngest brother-in-law, Vivek, as her own child. Mrs Bansal's Dhruv was in twelfth standard, preparing for both the school board and engineering entrance exams. Maya's middle daughter, Nalini, was one year his senior, like Vivek. Last year, they had both prepared for their medical and engineering exams respectively and had both failed to get through. While Vivek had been sent to a private college, Nalini had enrolled in a Bachelor of Arts degree in the local college and was preparing for her second attempt this year. Maya's youngest daughter, Naina, was two years younger than Nalini. She had topped her high school board exams. Now the neighbourhood was turning blue holding its breath to see what subject she would choose in eleventh standard.

When they heard about the plate, they convened at the Kapoor house the same evening. They scrutinised the disappearance from every angle, considering all possibilities. Maya gave Mahima a full hearing but firmly ruled out Pushpa, saying she did not have the brains to do something like this. She asked who else had been inside the house that morning. Mrs Bansal asked what the plate was worth. Mahima went through their lines of inquiry zealously while Sumi sat with them, adding information wherever she could. No one had entered the house that morning, narrowing down the possibilities to an inconvenient few. They too agreed that the plate wouldn't have gone anywhere and would turn up inside the house sooner than later. Although she wasn't convinced, Mahima felt suitably attended to and they reverted to talking about their children.

"Neeti is so busy with her internship, she doesn't have time to visit us, even to meet prospective grooms," Maya said. "Says 'you can choose' – can you believe that?! Nalini is lost in her books. As for Naina, she's always angry. I'm scared of saying anything to her, she will only go and do exactly the opposite. Sumi, dear, will you talk to her? You have so many degrees, she might listen to you."

"And while you're at it, Sumi, can you tutor Dhruv in maths? He barely passed in the unit test last week," Mrs Bansal piped in.

Sumi looked at Mahima. She had no desire to impinge upon this sorority. Equally, she did not want to offend them. All she wanted to do was go to her room and work on her application. Yet here she was, having an extended afternoon tea, going over the missing plate yet another time and debating subject choices of the neighbours' children.

Mahima was looking at her too. "Of course, why not! That is one thing our Sumi knows very well," she said with a smile that made it impossible to tell if it was a compliment or a complaint.

Sumi found herself agreeing, as her alleged extended family closed in on her.

The Language of Love

Sixteen was hardly out of the playground of childhood, but Naina conducted her life with the worn-out weariness of an adult. She had been doing so as far back as anyone could recall. She was a girl in a rush. She did not have time to learn everything through her own mistakes, and had realised early on that if she observed the people around her keenly, they were generous with lessons on what *not* to do.

Naina was walking home after making some deliveries for her mother when she saw Chhotu, Pushpa's son, running away from three older boys who looked about ten or eleven years old. She crossed the road to intercept him and asked what the matter was. The bigger boys were playing seven stones with a cricket ball, but instead of aiming at the seven stones, the target was him. With her forefinger, she commanded the boys to come to her. They dithered. Two ran away, while the last one, their leader, stood still. Naina walked over to him, extended her hand for the ball and told him that if he or his minions even so much as came near Chhotu, their next game would be with her and the target would be their balls.

He gulped and scooted as fast as his legs would carry him. She gave the cricket ball to Chhotu and continued on her way.

It was the deadline to submit the form for her secondary school subject to the admin office today. Her school had recently introduced commerce as an option for secondary. It was an entirely new road that opened up an entirely new world for people who aspired to be neither doctors nor engineers, but chartered accountants, company secretaries and MBAs. Most parents did not know what the abbreviation stood for and thought a secretary was someone who took dictations, typed letters and made chai. But then came stories of someone who knew someone whose nephew got a job with an MNC, another abbreviation, with a starting salary of twenty thousand rupees, post-tax, and some of that scorn turned into awe. In the first year, the section had twenty students, but by the next, it had swelled into a class of sixty. Naina heard that accounting companies offered internships to commerce and economics undergraduates, with a possibility of permanent placement after graduation and a subsidy for an MBA if you signed a five-year bond. Admissions for university became more and more competitive, the cut-offs crawling up every year, but acing exams was child's play to her – even if she didn't care much about the subject.

When Naina announced she was thinking of taking commerce, Maya had been livid.

"You have ninety-two per cent! They will roll out the red carpet for you in the maths section," she said.

Naina shrugged.

"At least take bio. What face am I going to show people?"

"Any. You have so many."

"Look at Sumi. Already a postgraduate, now preparing for a doctorate. Kapoor aunty can barely contain her pride."

"And yet, here she is, making chai, just like the rest of you."

Maya shook her head. "A world of possibilities staring at you and you want to squander it away. Just like your father," the last line was muttered under her breath, but was loud enough for Naina to hear.

Her recollection of her childhood was a patchwork of memories of her father. Her earliest clear memory was from when she was seven. There used to be big dinners at home for his work friends. Sometimes they came with their families, but mostly it was just the uncles. She remembered helping her mother place dish after dish on the dining table, until there was no more space. Then they pulled the cane coffee table next to it for more dishes that kept flowing out of the kitchen. Maya was not an exceptional cook, but she made up for this by preparing dishes that the guests were partial to. Kumar uncle loved chicken, as did Naina herself. He was the boss. He came in a black Ambassador car and brought 5Star chocolate bars for Naina, Nalini and Neeti each time he visited. She was in second standard then. She used to save half the chocolate for her best friend.

She remembered going to the riverside on Sundays on her father's bicycle. Neeti and Nalini both on the girls' cycle and she on the front bar of her father's. The wind blew her hair onto her father's face. He was a tall man and smelled of tobacco. He carried a pouch of tobacco leaves in his shirt pocket and rolled his own cigarettes. On these trips, they took sketch books and water paints, sat outside the abandoned mazaar and painted all morning. Naina was a natural at painting. She did portraits. People said there was something remarkable about the eyes she painted. They followed the viewer, whichever angle they were seen from. Nalini liked to sketch the plants and laboured over their shape, size and the lines that crisscrossed over the leaves. Neeti watched animals. And Bhaskar spoke to them. He whistled to the birds, and they whistled back. He said that if you listened carefully, you could understand what every creature said. The birds were saying that they were happy to see them.

When he was happy, he spoke fast. He had wanted to be a veterinary doctor as a child, but he was the eldest and had to start earning soon, so he took up the first job that came his way, which was with a local builder. He did everything he was asked to, from filing papers to making chai to helping with designs. It turned out that he was exceptionally good at design, which became his bread and butter. Naina once asked him if that made him sad. As long as he was with his daughters, he said, nothing could make him sad.

Often on their way back, Naina would fall asleep on

the cycle. She would slide to the end of the bar and lean against his chest as he rode, and when she opened her eyes, she'd be in her bed. She now wondered how her father managed the ride back.

By the time she was in fourth standard, the dinners dwindled, with the exception of Kumar uncle who continued to visit. Sometimes Naina heard her parents quarrel. She did too much, he'd say. She did it for the family, she'd reply.

Bhaskar spent more and more hours at work. His company won a housing complex tender near the coast at the other end of the country. They needed a designer on the ground. The transfer came with significant perks. At home, the fights became louder. Naina would stand outside her parents' bedroom door, catching broken sentences.

"Chicken every week?"

"You need to take the offer."

"It's fifteen hours by train. I won't see you and the girls for months."

"We need other things too, slightly more important than seeing each other."

"We're a family, let us all go together."

"And raise them in a village?"

She remembered that her tenth birthday fell on a Saturday. That Sunday, her father took them for what she later realised would be their last excursion. He brought along a set of oil paints and canvases.

"Try this," he said. He called Naina "gudiya", his doll.

Neither of them were very good with the oil paints. They produced dead, patchy paintings.

"Why are we using these? I like water paints," Naina complained.

"Because water paints don't allow you to make mistakes. With these, you can paint over as many times as you like."

That night, as the girls lay in their bed, he sat between them and placed his hands on their heads. He had accepted the transfer. It came with a promotion and a raise. He would come home every month and bring presents for the girls. He would bring a forty-eight shades paint set for Naina. Naina felt like someone had punched her in the gut and knocked the air out of her lungs. She couldn't breathe. She could not imagine being without her father for a single day. She could not believe he was saying this, let alone doing this.

"I don't want paints. I want you," she said.

"I'm going for your and your sisters' sake, gudiya," he said. "You are the love of my life." The words came out very slowly.

She remembered counting days till the month's end. He visited regularly the first few months. She remembered every little detail of those days, and absolutely nothing of the weeks that passed in between. Then came month ends when he did not show up. She remembered swinging at the gate, waiting for a rickshaw to turn into their street. She asked her mother why he did not visit every month. Maya told her to be grateful for what she had, for such questions occurred in one's head only when one's belly was full.

Naina was used to the runny, wilful water paints. She did not get along with the thick blobs of oil paints that sat there, waiting to be told where to go. She gave up painting. She took her collection of artwork to the local general merchant and struck a deal with him to sell them for fifty paise a piece, for a 10 per cent commission. She checked in with him every day. After a month, she brought home all the paintings except one that the shopkeeper bought for forty-five paise.

Maya started a tiffin service. There was no fixed menu. She cooked whatever her customers asked her to, but there was chicken every Wednesday. Some days, as she walked home from her school bus, Naina saw a black Ambassador drive away. Those days were always Wednesdays.

When she was fourteen, a student brought roller skates to school. Naina had never seen anything like it and wanted a pair too. They cost seven hundred rupees and Maya refused. They simply did not have that kind of money. Naina made a deal that instead of the rickshaw wallah, she would deliver all meals for Maya's tiffin service, for the "rest of her life" in exchange for the skates. The skates were ill-suited to the cobbly streets of Shantinagar, but Naina persisted and found a way to bend her knees, shift her weight from this leg to that leg and swerve around the stones and potholes. She made good her promise willingly. With every passing year, her remit of errands increased. She collected empty containers from customers, took their orders, kept the books and deposited cheques in the bank. There came a day when even Maya had to agree that they were even. From then on, she got paid five rupees a month for doing odd jobs for the house. She kept the money locked in a large aluminium trunk under her bed and hid the key.

"What are you going to do with all this money?" Maya asked her.

"Buy a one-way ticket to the other end of the country," she said, staring into her mother's eyes, long and hard.

Every month there was a credit of four thousand rupees in Maya's passbook. According to Naina's calculations, it was more than sufficient to cover the bills, groceries and school fees. But Maya continued with her tiffin service. It had started with a few orders for snacks and sweets during Diwali, Eid, Christmas and Holi but gradually expanded into a full-fledged business. She cooked what her customers wanted and exactly how they wanted it. When people asked her the secret of her cooking, she said there wasn't any. There was no one right way of cooking a dish. Even a dal was only as good as it tasted to the person for whom it was made. She made efforts to learn how the husbands and children liked their food. She remembered birthdays, anniversaries and sent surprise sweets for them.

Naina was repulsed. "People have let you in on their dining tables, doesn't mean you slither into their lives."

"You cannot be in one and not in the other," Maya replied.

The house smelled of onions and oil. Soon the smell was in Naina's clothes and her hair and wouldn't go away, no matter how much she washed. The air in the house was thick with it. She began to spend more time out of it than in.

One such day, she took her father's bicycle and rode to the river on her own. The ride was long and hot. Her hair did not fly in the wind because there was no wind. Instead, it stuck to her ears with sweat. When she reached the riverside, she did not recognise the place. The riverbed was dry. The mazaar looked more derelict than before, the vines that once adorned it like a scarf going in and out and around now hung like cobwebs. Everything was quiet. She chirruped to the birds in the trees. They stared back at her with poker faces, mocking her for believing that they had ever spoken to her.

The only sound she heard was a rustling in the bushes. She followed it and peered into the tall, spiky grass to find two yellow eyes glinting back at her. They belonged to a puppy. She extended her hand. He backed away. She took a Parle-G biscuit from her bag, broke it into small pieces and put it down. The puppy sniffed them, tried to get them in its mouth, but the more he tried, the further he nudged them away. Eventually he gave up and closed his eyes. Naina picked him up and brought him back home.

Maya wouldn't allow him in the house. "This is a home, not a dharamshala that any stray can walk in."

"Of course," said Naina. "Only the ones you allow."

She took him to the market, bought a packet of full cream milk and poured it into his mouth drop by drop. Chhotu said he would take him home. They named him Sheru – the tiger.

※

The shopkeepers in the colony knew Naina by name. She bought a cigarette from the paan wallah whenever she went to buy betel leaves for her mother. At first, he refused to sell it to her. He had seen her since she was a baby and thought of her like a daughter. He acquiesced only because she threatened to buy it from the next market. Even so, each time he slipped a cigarette to her, hidden under the pack of leaves, he made her promise that it would be the last. She nodded, acknowledging his concern. She slipped out at night, after everyone retired to their rooms, walked to the back of the house and sat under the ledge of the kitchen window to smoke. The back of her house faced the backs of the Kapoors' and Bansals' houses, making a triangle. From where she sat, she could see both their bedroom windows on the first floor.

Vivek's window was dark now. The previous year, it used stay lit till early mornings as he studied for the engineering entrance exams. Then, a few months ago, it had started blinking, slowly and randomly at first, and then seemed to acquire a language of its own. A language spoken by him and one other person, which was all a language needed to survive, two people to speak it. Naina came here to this dark, quiet corner for a few moments of escape from her world and found that she had trespassed into another world that spoke in light. When she realised who were talking and what was being said, she intercepted and put a stop to the conversation. She had not imagined though that when the lights went out in Vivek's room, they would go out from his heart too. Her father had been wrong. Some creatures went totally quiet. Especially in their direst moments, when they should be screaming for help, they went mute. No sound came out of them, no matter how hard you listened.

※

Now Naina was a sixteen-year-old girl of full proportions and ruddy complexion. People said she looked like her father. Like most people her age, she could not wait to leave Shantinagar. Unlike most people her age, she did not much care how she did it.

There was Nalini, by far the prettiest girl in the locality, a younger version of Maya and the fancy of many a boy. She could not be bothered to acknowledge it, but this only added to her charm. Her big eyes hid behind thick-rimmed spectacles and her thick, unmade brows strained towards each other, pondering over physics problems. Her long hair was plaited, twisted and confined to a tight bun. Soon after their father left, Nalini decided that she wanted to become a doctor and had been preparing for the entrance exams ever since. She was the type who had to work hard for each mark, unlike Naina, who did not need to open her notebook after the teacher went through a lesson and still stayed at the top of her class. Nalini had failed to make it to a good medical college in her first attempt. Now she punished herself by attending Bachelor of Arts classes by day and medical coaching classes in the afternoons.

Then there was Neeti. She had taken after Maya too, but unlike Nalini, whose features had blossomed and come into their own, Neeti's had refused. They were frozen in time, perhaps sometime around when she was fourteen, with thin lips and small eyes, making her forehead look even bigger than it already was. Over the years, Naina had watched her oldest sister fold in on herself over and over, becoming smaller and smaller, on a mission to disappear. The rumours about her being an illegitimate child were an open secret. All of Shantinagar knew about them, everyone had a view on what was really the truth, but no one said a word to her. They hung over her like a cloud, following her wherever she went, to school, to the market and inside the house. So, she sat on the last bench in class where no one could see her or her cloud, and at home she ate quickly and retreated to her room and stayed there as long as she could. The moment she finished twelfth, she managed to get an internship in Delhi with *The Times* and left. Whatever she saved after paying for her hostel fees and food, she sent home like she was in a rush to repay some kind of debt. Every time she came home, Maya asked what her plans were. Neeti didn't have any.

"If you wish, we can find someone for you," Mrs Bansal said. She had already spoken to two good families about her. Neeti looked at the pictures of the two boys as Mrs Bansal described their families and houses.

"What do you think?" Maya asked her.

Neeti shrugged.

"What am I supposed to do with that? It's for you, you need to choose."

"She must be feeling shy," Mrs Bansal said understandingly. She turned to Neeti. "The superintendent's family is good but, if you ask me, the sari store people will be better. They'll stay here as long as they live, no job transfers, no politicians visiting home. Plus, this one has a younger brother. Who knows, maybe Nalini or even Naina ... What say, Naina?"

Naina clapped her hands in prayer, joined them to her forehead and said, "Spare me, please."

"There's no rush," Mrs Bansal continued. "Think about it. They want an answer by next week. They are talking to other families too. And bring me two pictures, one full and one close up."

Naina went with Neeti to the studio. The photographer tried to get her to smile or to at least look happy but gave up. They came home with pictures of her staring blankly into the camera.

"What have you decided?" Naina asked her.

"Both are okay. Ma can decide," she said.

"What are you trying to do? Is this some kind of repentance?" Naina asked.

Neeti didn't respond.

"Whatever happened, it's not your fault! You don't have to sacrifice your happiness for someone else's deeds," she said, looking at her mother. "It will solve nothing."

"Slave your life away for your children and this is how they talk to you. Go give this to Dhruv," Maya said, handing a container of sweet, orange, red and green rice to Naina. "Tell him I made it specially for his birthday."

"You made this for the Eid get-together for number fourteen."

"Yes, but I made extra for him. He likes it."

"Then say that. Why lie?"

"This isn't lying."

"Then what is it?"

"If you tell him the whole story, the rice will not be special anymore."

"It isn't."

"What is the point of fussing over the right words if they don't say what we want them to? Words work for us, not us for them."

"The whole world revolves for you. I'm out of here."

"Keep the bag straight, I've garnished it with raisins on top. He likes raisins."

Naina realised that her father had been wrong on that too. No one did anything for anyone. People chased their own dreams. They did what their hearts desired, all the time trying to pin it on other people, trying to convince them that it was all being done for them.

So that afternoon, when class eleven entrants lined up at school to turn in their forms with their preferred subjects, it was with a crystal-clear mind that she ticked commerce.

Arrow of Time

Naina's decision sent shockwaves through Shantinagar. It was all anybody could talk about. Mahima heard from at least three families whose children had checked commerce simply because Naina had, and Mrs Bansal reported that four students from Dhruv's batch, one year Naina's senior, had gone to the admin office to ask if they could change their subject retrospectively, a year into biology or mathematics, Dhruv being one of them. They promised they would cover all of last year's syllabus before school reopened, how much harder could it be compared with slogging through unpronounceable Latin words and inscrutable theorems. This year saw the largest intake so far for commerce. The school would need more teachers, perhaps even take the next-door classroom from biology and shift them to the new library wing. Maya was fed up with answering people as to why Naina had done this. The trio asked Sumi what she thought about it.

Sumi liked Naina. She admired how, at sixteen, Naina knew her mind clearly and was going through life on her own terms. Naina was what Sumi had always thought herself to be, but here they both were, one who had gone and decided for herself, while Sumi had not written a word beyond the title of her proposed dissertation. Every time she sat down with her writing pad and pen, something or the other came up to distract her. Or was she distracting herself from the fact that she had always imagined that her father, Professor Diwakar, would be by her side as she wrote her application, standing over her shoulder, guiding her, correcting her, and that, without him, she was floundering?

What would she say to Naina? Bold as it was, a person of Naina's intellect opting for commerce was a poor decision, statistically speaking. It was like an outlier trying to crawl its way back inside the bell curve. Or using a cauldron to boil a cup of tea, as Mahima might put it. She wished she could explain this to Naina. Schools gave a month's grace period, in case students changed their minds. But people like Naina rarely did. Sumi knew the type a bit too well.

Sumi's father taught physics in Allahabad University. Her mother, Lalita, taught in the local municipality primary school. Her main subject was Hindi, but she could as easily dip into English, maths or science if a class was lagging in any syllabus. Sumi's brother, Gyan, was two years younger than her. They lived in the staff quarters on the university campus, surrounded by other faculty members. The buildings were old but comfortable. Theirs was a two-bedroom house that was furnished simply, with only the things that were needed. In the few hours that she got to be at home, Lalita kept it spotlessly clean. Often when she had extra classes, they ordered food from the hostel canteen.

All four of them loved a good argument. It was the staple conversation at dinner. Professor Diwakar was wont to throw a controversial statement at the table and then sit back and watch with pleasure how the others tore it apart. He started this as a way to enrich Sumi and Gyan's knowledge when they were young. His days in college were long and he did not get to spend as much time with the children as he would have liked. This was his way of sharpening their curiosity and opening up different lines of inquiry. Over the years, however, this became their primary way of engaging with each other. Each developed an individual style of arguing. Professor Diwakar was instigator-in-chief. He set the agenda for discussion, usually with a provocative statement, and let the children pounce at it, coming in occasionally to add an insight that would take the level of discussion up a notch. Sumi was the logical thinker. She read voraciously and entered these discussions with data and quotes. Gyan was not much of a reader, but he did not let that come in the way of tabling his opinions, which were, for the most part, the opposite of Sumi's. He was no match for her intellectually. His arsenal comprised of red-herring fallacies, emotional appeals and just about any other trick that could help him win over his sister, or at least bring the discussion to a stalemate. As time went by, Sumi's reading and style of thinking came to mirror her father's and the two of them became a unified front, corroborating each other's thoughts more than arguing. The more they colluded, the more aggressive Gyan became. Every time he was unable to poke holes in their rock-solid reasoning, he went into spirals of illogical assertions, often tuning out of the discussion and ending up sulking, while father and daughter went deeper and deeper into the issue. Lalita, although fully capable, chose not to enter these discussions head on. Instead, she liked to throw curve balls from entirely unexpected quarters. She was also the timekeeper. As much as she respected her husband's instructive dialogue, it did interfere with her meticulous planning of the evenings. The children needed to pack their school bags and lay out their uniforms for the next morning and get to bed on time.

"Will you keep talking or is there any plan to finish dinner too? Look, the dal has gone cold."

"Completely right, Lalitaji," Professor Diwakar said, with an aggressive nod, approving and agreeing. That was not the response she was expecting, but then she had come to expect the unexpected from her husband.

"You can tell that time has passed because the dal that was warm is now cold," he continued.

"Entropy!" Sumi said. "The arrow of time." She had just finished reading Reichenbach's *The Direction of Time* and couldn't wait to flaunt.

Professor Diwakar beamed at her.

"What?" Gyan asked.

"Left to their own, systems fall to a lower order as

time passes. They become worse. That is how we can say that time has moved forward."

Gyan stared at her, trying to grasp the concept and come up with a counter-response simultaneously, without letting any of it show.

"Like your room. The longer you stay in it, the messier it becomes. Get it?"

"What if things don't go bad? The clock still moves on, right?" he said.

"He has a point, Professor Saab," Lalita said. She knew Gyan was punching far above his weight just to be contrary. "Some things get better with time. What happens to your theory then?"

"Like what?" Sumi asked.

"Like relationships. Take this family. We have more fun with each other now than when it was just your father and me."

"Yes, but you see, Lalitaji, the system has to be a closed system. A family is not a closed system."

"See this is what always happens. Your theories duck behind exceptions every time we start talking about the real things."

"What about mangoes?" Gyan asked. "They get sweeter just lying around."

"They are open systems too, living things."

"No, they are not. After they have been plucked from the tree, they are not."

Sumi lived for these dinner conversations. She particularly enjoyed beating Gyan. He was an electron, a minuscule dot, flitting from here to there, taking a stance only when they asked him to, just like how an electron's location could be pinned down only when it was measured. Before measurement it was nothing but a probability curve of many possible locations. Some quantum physicists went as far as to say that an electron's reality did not matter until the point when it was measured, that it did not really exist until someone tried to see it. She saw him dodging under Baba's questions, jumping over her points, a noise in their carefully laid-out data that she could not get rid of. A part of her felt sorry for her brother. Science was not his love. He was a history and literature boy. These discussions that started in science and ambled into philosophy did not tickle him. But he was too proud to sit them out. He insisted on jumping in and ended up defeated and sullen. Somewhere on the periphery of her vision, Sumi could see him drifting away from her. She knew that if she reached out, as an elder sister, she could make things better between them. But the temptation to prove her intellectual superiority and impress Baba pulled her to the other side each time. With every lost debate, Gyan grew more hostile and the distance between them widened.

Professor Diwakar was a quiet atheist. He accompanied his family and friends to places of worship whenever called upon. To his companions he was affable and to the gods he was respectful. But to him, these visits were expeditions in data collection. Sumi knew this because she was his assistant in this. They went as ethnographers, collecting observations to prove his hypotheses. Every place of worship he visited served to strengthen his belief that the raison d'être of religion was to create fear. Fear of mortality drove people to believe in superpowers controlling their lives that could be moved by supplication. He had concluded that the creator, maintainer and destroyer were not somewhere in the exosphere or under the sea, but right here, amongst us. That there was no accountant with a thick curly moustache, decked in jewels, sitting in heaven with a large register, chalking up our sins and good deeds in red and green ink, feeding them into a complex algorithm that determined whether we came back to Earth as worm or human. Darwin's theory, as slow and devoid of magic as it was, was all there was. We come to Earth with genes passed on to us by our parents, spend our lives advancing our survival skills and pass on those genes, hopefully smarter and stronger, to the next generation. Lalita's views were similar to her husband's, yet not the same. She too did not believe in the powers of prayer, only in action. She did right, gave her best to everything she did and braced herself for the worst. Pouring her 100 per cent into whatever she did, be it correcting student homework or scrubbing the dishes, was the closest she came to praying. Yet, she did not allow herself to believe that there were no powers governing life. As far as the scientific community was concerned, the jury was still out on this and she made space for that uncertainty. Partly out of scientific rigour and partly, she admitted openly, for sheer survival, for what if, just in case, there *was* someone, watching from above the clouds? She did not want to get on their wrong side. So her temple visits were a shade more involved than her husband's. When she visited a temple, she mouthed the mantras. She insisted that her children learn the gayatri mantra by heart and know what each Sanskrit word meant. Sumi found this ambiguous, even hypocritical. The fuzzy borders of her mother's beliefs were nowhere as elegant as the sharp edges of her father's black-and-white arguments. Professor Diwakar was generally tolerant of Lalita's approach, but there were moments when their differences came to the fore.

"Why are you teaching them things you yourself don't believe in, Lalitaji?"

"I'm not asking them to believe in it. But they need to know."

"For what?"

"To decide whether they want to believe in it or not."

"You and I can tell them that," he said, "and save them precious years. It takes entire lifetimes for people to realise that this is all bunkum."

"You talk as if this is some chapter out of your syllabus, and we need to sit them down for a lesson."

"It is what I believe to be true."

"That's what I'm saying. It is your belief, let them find theirs."

By fourteen, Sumi was so imbued in her father's way of thinking that she adopted his atheism with full conviction. Gyan, therefore, went all out to defend the gods.

Whenever he attended a prayer ceremony, he kept the saffron thread on his wrist for days, until the colour ran out and all that remained was a worn thread of a dubious light-brown shade. From the vast catalogue of gods, he chose Hanuman, the monkey god who had sworn lifelong allegiance to Lord Rama. He learned all forty verses of the *Hanuman Chalisa* and began to fast every Tuesday. At some level, Sumi knew that this was just his way of asserting his individuality in the house, though she was convinced that he was mistaken and wanted better for him. But their camps were too clearly delineated by now. There was no longer room for a heart-to-heart talk. Every conversation was a continuation of some old debate, every sentence a point scored, or not.

Unable to speak directly to him, Sumi vented to her mother that Gyan was being stupid.

Lalita heard her patiently. "It is a long road that he is walking down. Let him find his way."

What she left unsaid was that Sumi had taken a short cut, following her father's footsteps. Clouded in indignation, the subtlety of this insinuation was lost on Sumi.

When she was eighteen, Sumi had clearly charted out her plan for further education. With her stellar performance in twelfth standard, admission to Bachelor of Science in the state college would be easy. She would then do a master's degree, followed by a PhD. Her thesis would be "Determinism versus Free Will: Lessons from an electron". She would prove that Newtonian laws eventually succumbed to laws that governed quantum particles. She was already researching the topic, making notes and creating a bibliography that she would need to get through to write her application.

When she was in the last year of her master's degree, Professor Diwakar had a heart attack. He was hospitalised for four days. Those were the longest four days of Sumi's life. She was suddenly made aware of her father's mortality. She put her life on hold, missed college and stayed by his side all through. It was a mild attack and, after running several tests, the doctor assured them that he had many years of healthy life ahead and discharged him. It was only when they got back home that Sumi felt she could breathe again. But even as she went back to college and her normal life resumed, she saw that the incident had changed Professor Diwakar. He started preparing for what he called "the return journey". He changed his diet to eat only home-cooked, plain and boiled food and started going for long walks. He cut down the number of classes he taught and devoted more of his time to reading. One evening, there was a box of sweets on the table, a gift from a colleague, for his son's marriage. Everyone partook of them except him.

"Which one is better, a short, happy life or a long, dull one?" Gyan asked, helping himself to the second laddoo.

"Good question," Professor Diwakar said.

"If it helps you live longer, then why not . . . ?" Sumi started, but she knew she was on shaky ground even before she had completed her sentence.

"How can you be sure of longevity? You cannot even tell where an electron is at any point in time, how do you say how long anyone is going to live?" Gyan shot back.

"One can try," Sumi replied.

"So you would give up assured and immediate happiness in the hope that doing so will allow you to live one more day, which you can spend staying away from happiness? And in the end, if you are lucky, you will have a long life devoid of pleasure? And there's no guarantee that doing this will actually help you live longer. Everything is a probability curve, isn't it?"

"As long as it is non-zero, it's worth it," Sumi said.

"Then you won't mind this," Gyan said, taking the laddoo from her hand and placing the whole thing into his mouth.

Professor Diwakar stayed out of this debate and out of most other things. He no longer indulged Sumi in her requests to borrow extra books from the library on his faculty card. He listened to her plans for her thesis but did not proffer his opinion. He said that they would discuss all the details together, but after she "settled down," a genteel term for getting married. Sumi was taken by surprise. She had known that marriage would happen to her at some point, simply because most adults that she knew were married. It had always seemed like an inevitable rite of passage, but she did not think of it as an important or necessary milestone. It threw a big spanner in the way that she had planned out her life. For once,

THE LIGHTS OF SHANTINAGAR

Sumi was not in full agreement with her father. She had her application ready. All she needed was her father and his colleague who taught quantum to whet it. Her physics professor would write her recommendation letter in the middle of the night, if she asked. This was the best place, and time, to apply. She had everything lined up. The whole marriage business would set her back at least one year, if not more. They would have to find the right match, go through the ceremonies, she would have to move to another house, maybe another city. How would her plans for a PhD work then? But her father's only response was, "They will."

Sumi had always trusted him, and this time was no different. Her faith in her father shushed the dissident voices in her head. As pointless as marriage sounded, she started thinking about it, just because it had come from him.

Lalita continued to ask her how she wanted to plan her studies. A few years of teaching experience would bode well for the doctorate application. Sumi was taken by surprise again that someone other than her father was taking a keen interest in her academic dreams. Now that she had accepted the decision to get married and internalised it, her mother's concerned questions felt like irritating naggings by someone who was not in on the plan. She sided with her father in thwarting her own dreams and began to look at Lalita as an outsider.

After she finished her master's, she took up teaching in the undergraduate college, while Professor Diwakar looked for suitable families for her. He first vetted the prospective grooms himself and then invited them home for tea for the customary meeting between the two families. During these visits, Lalita made sure to mention Sumi's plans for a doctorate and scanned their faces for reactions. The reactions ranged from bemused smiles to incredulity to outright laughter. After the guests left, the four of them sat around, discussing the match and finishing up the snacks. Gyan found the whole exercise ludicrous. During these post-mortems, he imitated the families and offered his take on what they said and what they really meant. His imitations were accurate and his interpretations annoying. Upon hearing of Sumi's doctorate plans, one potential mother-in-law had said, "Yes, yes, why not?" and laughed a loud, forced laugh. When she'd left, Gyan mimicked her Punjabi accent and finished the sentence for her: "And after that, we will fly you to America for whatever degree people do after a PhD, okay?"

"Of course, of course. She is as much our daughter as she is yours," actually meant, "Don't worry Professor Saab, you've managed to keep her out of this madness so far, we'll take it from here."

"Really? What for, beta?" was the only one for which Gyan had no wisecrack.

"At least they are honest," he said.

Sumi ignored him and turned to her father. "What do you say, Baba?"

"He's saying, 'Do whatever you want but get off my head first'," Gyan supplied.

Meeting all these families made Sumi's heart sink. She did not like any of the prospective grooms. The boys hardly spoke. Conversations were usually led by the parents and revolved around her cooking and housekeeping skills. Professor Diwakar listened to everyone's analysis of the families but said little. Lalita was more vocal in her disapproval of the families. They met seven families before she dug out their connections to a boy named Dev. He was a former student of Professor Diwakar's and had been to their house a few times. She invited him over for tea, for which he came alone.

He was tall and slim. Sumi couldn't help noticing his long nose and his pronounced Adam's apple. He asked if he could speak with Sumi in private, and they went down for a walk. She told him about her PhD. He said Professor Diwakar was such an inspiring teacher it was no surprise that his daughter had inherited the same love for learning. He too had wanted to study further after his BSc, he said.

"Why didn't you?" Sumi asked.

"I'm the middle of three brothers." His voice was throaty. "Papa retired two years ago. Om bhaiyya is a businessman; he has good days and bad days. And he has two little boys. My younger brother just started engineering. We needed a steady income to support the family."

Sumi had been so fired up on her dreams, it hadn't occurred to her that further studies was a privilege not everyone had access to.

"You do your PhD," Dev said. "I will feel like I'm doing it."

His only request was that he wanted to live with his parents and look after them. This was an unusual request because it was what families did anyway. They took care of the previous generation while creating the next one. Grandparents helped raise the grandchildren while the children went about feeding everyone. It masqueraded as many things – as culture, tradition, filial duty, even love – but what it was, was a custody of the family's genes, carefully passed from one generation to another. As a general rule, after marriage the bride would move in with her in-laws. It showed that Dev had, at least for a few moments, entertained the notion of living away from his parents on his would-be-wife's account. It was a different matter that he had come to the same conclusion as everyone else. His shared love for science and thoughtfulness made him shine above the rest.

"What's your verdict on this one?" Sumi asked Gyan after Dev left. It was a dare for him to say something that would go against everyone else.

"I don't know. Looks all right. Anyway, since when do you need permission from strangers to do what you want?"

"I don't," she snapped. Once again, Gyan had her and both of them knew it.

"Isn't that what this parade is all about?"

"I don't need anyone's permission to do what I want!"

"Yes, you do. Because, in this house, Baba won't give it to you."

Lalita lay her hand on Gyan's thigh gently. It was his cue to stop. He knew he had won this one even before it was over. Sumi was close to tears. It wouldn't take much to get them out. But he let it go.

He started clearing up. Lalita helped him. Professor Diwakar rose and went to his room. Sumi kept sitting, fuming and confused.

The wedding was a simple affair. Lalita made it clear to Mrs Kapoor that there would be no dowry, not because they could not afford it but because it went against every value that they stood for.

"We are giving you our most prized possession. She will bring prosperity to your home with her hard work," Lalita said.

Mrs Kapoor said this was well enough, because they wouldn't accept any dowry anyway. "We will look after your daughter as our own," she said.

There were modest presents for every member of the Kapoor family, saris for the ladies, suit pieces for the men and boys. Sumi took all her possessions with her in three suitcases, filled with new clothes, the little gold that Lalita had amassed for her, some books and her draft application. Gyan came to drop her off in Shantinagar. Before leaving, he handed her a book. It was a heavily underlined copy of *What Is Life? The Physical Aspect of the Living Cell* by Erwin Schrödinger. The last page of the book was folded at the top corner, and the last sentence double underlined:

Arrow of Time

What is this "I"? It is just the canvas on which data (experiences and memories) are collected ... And even if a skilled hypnotist succeeded in blotting out entirely all your earlier reminiscences, you would not find that he had killed you. In no case is there a loss of personal existence to deplore. Nor will there ever be.

❁

Settling into her in-laws' house turned out to be easier than Sumi had expected. Of course, the plate's disappearance had left a bitter taste, but even that hadn't come in the way of the family embracing her wholeheartedly. Not once did Mummyji and Daddyji question her doctorate plans. On the contrary, they asked her about it with a mix of awe and curiosity, like people trying to decode a piece of abstract art. Om, whose network of acquaintances had long reaches, made a standing offer to Sumi to find a connection in whichever department of the university she chose. Vivek, the younger brother-in-law, had come for three days, just for the wedding. He was a younger version of Dev. The same slim build, long nose and the same Adam's apple. Luv and Kush were delirious to have their uncle back, and were then miserable that he had to leave again. They found their new aunt an acceptable substitute in the meantime. The only person who was less than warm to Sumi was Mahima. She clearly considered Sumi a rival who had come to challenge her heretofore unencumbered reign over the kitchen and the household. Sumi wanted to tell her that she need not worry, that she had neither the skills nor the desire to prove anything in the kitchen. She had married so that she could get on with her PhD and was happy to let Mahima hold on to her little fiefdom forever. But she could not find the right opportunity or words to say this without sounding callous to her or the family.

Dev stayed true to his word. He helped her unpack her suitcases and made sure she had everything she needed in the house. He even bought a study lamp and put it on the bedside table near her. He did not make any overtures to consummate the marriage. On their first night, he picked up his pillow and sheet and offered to sleep on the floor.

"There's no need to be so filmi," Sumi said, moving closer to her edge of the bed to make room for him. Dev considered this for a moment and sat back on the bed, as close to his edge as he could. There was enough space in the middle of the bed to accommodate a whole other person. He placed a bolster there: a big one, about half the length of the bed. The cover was a block print of red elephants, their outline embroidered in a simple line-stitch of green thread.

"What is this now?" Sumi asked.

"Quantum physics," he said, and they both laughed. It was Dev's way of keeping his promise to her.

The bolster gave Sumi much comfort. It became a permanent resident on their bed. At night, when everyone retired to their rooms, the new couple caught up with each other's day, from the safety of their respective sides.

Sumi liked to stroke the red elephants. They listened to everything that was said in the room.

※

"What do you think?" she asked the elephants. "Did Naina make the right choice for her future?"

They side-eyed her, as if to say, "How about we talk about your future first?"

Adequately chastised, Sumi picked up her application form. For a few minutes, her pen hovered under the title "Determinism versus Free Will: Lessons from an electron", but no words came out and her mind wandered. She lifted her pillow and pulled out a letter from underneath it.

She had received post a few days into the wedding. There were two letters, one from her mother and the other from her father. She read Lalita's letter first, which was written on school notebook paper in small, evenly shaped letters. She asked how Sumi was finding her new family and whether she was missing them back home. She enjoined her to keep an open mind in the new environment, reminding her to be respectful, fair and kind, even in adverse situations, of which there might be many, just because it was a new place and different people. Lalita regretted that she had not prepared Sumi well in housework and cooking and said that she should try to learn the ways of the house and help as best as she could. She offered to write to the office of the college in Shantinagar to enquire about teaching positions. Sumi speed-read the two pages and put them to one side. Then she leaned back on the bed, hugged the bolster and, together with the elephants, settled down to read her father's letter. It was a page from the same notebook, but with his scrawling cursive writing, illegible in parts.

My dear Sumati,

I am happy to hear that you are settling well in your new home. Here, the house feels empty without you. Gyan and I are having long discussions these days on theology. He is reading a translation of the Rig Ved and shared the Hymn of Creation with us. I am impressed and, I have to admit, surprised by the line of sceptical inquiry in such an ancient and religious text. He tries to fill in for you by conjecturing what you would have said for each argument. He gets quite close!

Upon the doctor's advice, I have started walking to and from college. Your mother is taking very good care of my diet.

I am confident that Dev will prove to be helpful in planning your next steps. I hear that the library in Shantinagar City College is not bad.

Best wishes,
Baba

She kept both letters under her pillow. She read the one from her father several times. She read it after she got ready in the morning, when she came back to her room after lunch and before retiring for the night. Something was missing. Like an electron whose probability curve suggested that it should be on that page, and yet defied detection repeatedly. After several rereads, she could neither find what was missing, nor could she say what it was.

Right and Wrong

One of Om's acquaintances was going to Allahabad and offered to carry anything Sumi wanted to send to her parents. She accepted the offer gratefully. She had been working on her application for the last few weeks and wanted her father to go through it. She got to work making a clean copy for him to review.

She did not hear from her father very much, although she wrote to him every other week. Replies came instead from her mother. She was reading one such letter on a sultry afternoon: Sumi's friend was getting married in November and one of Lalita's friends was a grandmother now. She asked Sumi how her class was and inquired about everyone at home. She included a recipe of besan laddoos for her to try. This irked Sumi. All those years, Lalita had kept Sumi out of the kitchen. She herself spent as little time cooking as she could get away with. They used to send Gyan to pack dinner from the hostel mess at least one day in the week because Lalita was held up at school for some extra class or the other. Now she expected her to roll laddoos in her in-laws' home?

Right and Wrong

"What does Ma say?" Mr Kapoor asked, in between slurps of tea.

"Nothing much. This and that."

"Four pages is a lot of this and that," he said.

"She's sent a recipe for laddoos."

"See! I knew you were hiding something. When can we have them?"

"I'm not a good cook, you know that. I've never made it, only helped Ma."

"Who does in their mother's house? I also learned after my marriage," Mrs Kapoor said.

"It's all my training. That's what she's trying to say," Mr Kapoor said.

"What I'm trying to say is, this is your house too. If you want to try," she said, pointing to the recipe.

The recipe stewed in her head for a few days and she finally decided to make it.

She chose an afternoon when Mahima and Mummyji were at Maya's house for tea. She could not imagine moving even a spatula in the kitchen without being corrected by Mahima. She took her mother's letter to the kitchen and gathered the ingredients. It made sense in the beginning: three cups of gram flour and three tablespoons of desi ghee. But it turned vague as it progressed. Two and a half to three cups of sugar. Three or four bulbs of green cardamom. Was she to put two and half or three, three or four? Trust Ma to send her off on a journey without a proper map. For a moment she wished she had done this with Mummyji. She would have told her how much to put without making her feel incompetent. But Sumi had chosen to do it by herself, so she did it the only way she knew. She measured out exactly two and three-quarter cups. When she warmed the ghee, the kitchen filled with the warm smell of cow-milk butter. Mixed with the roasted flour and sugar, it turned into a moist, sand-like sludge. From here onwards, she was on familiar ground. All she had to do now was take half a handful of the sludge and roll it into a sphere. She and Gyan had done this on the rare occasions when their mother made these at home. Sumi took carefully calibrated half handfuls of it and rolled it between her palms until there were perfect spheres, and then she rolled them some more, till a layer of ghee seeped out and gave the spheres a sticky sheen. She placed them in a steel container in equidistant concentric circles. When it was all done, she licked her fingers. She was pleasantly surprised at how close it came to what her mother made. She would have liked it a little sweeter, Gyan would have liked it much sweeter, but this was the correct level of sweetness for her father and Om bhaiyya.

Everyone liked the laddoos. The approval was so unanimous that even Mahima refrained from passing critical comments. They were offered like trophies to anyone who came to visit.

When Om's friend came to collect Sumi's parcel, she was ready with her application in a brown envelope. Mrs Kapoor brought out a new double bedsheet to send to Sumi's parents.

"Get four laddoos in a steel container," she said to Sumi.

"Why for them? Ma is the one who asked me to make it for you."

"She'll feel nice. She must be missing you."

A chuckle escaped Sumi. "Ma?! She is not like that."

"What is she like?" Mrs Kapoor asked, tilting her head, a hint of a smile on her face.

"Nothing." Sumi smiled back but did Mrs Kapoor's bidding.

※

Meanwhile, what Mahima could not say in critique of Sumi's laddoos, she compensated for in praise of someone else. She would often speak about the fortitude with which Maya had borne the rumours about Neeti, the ignominy of her husband's disappearance, how she had raised three daughters single-handedly, almost. About how she rose above the wagging tongues of the neighbourhood. Now she was arranging the much-talked-about daughter's wedding, all on her own.

The cash flow of Maya's house was still the fodder for many a conversation in Shantinagar. After people had gone through the routines of discussing each other's well-being, the failing health of their parents and their children's unsatisfactory performance in school, they turned to more interesting topics like how the young and beautiful Maya could run a house and manage three sets of school fees with her catering business alone, and now host a wedding on top of everything. Speculations ranged from the obvious, support from the estranged husband or a hidden pot of gold, to more colourful ones like generous clients and transactions that extended beyond food. It wasn't so much said as suggested, innuendos delicately stacked one upon another until a narrative took shape that moved with the wind, something you could smell but not touch; hard to miss but impossible to pin down exactly who had said what. There were as many conjectures as there were people, but the men always took a kinder view of Maya than they expected to, which made the women say meaner things than they intended to. But these idle ponderings were the domain of people who did not know her well. To her friends, she was the embodiment of emotional strength and financial acumen.

"And she is not even tenth pass," Mahima made sure to add.

Sumi felt the jab of this barb in all its sharpness, for she, with her postgraduate degree and a teaching job, did not make half as much.

In moments like these, Sumi found herself wondering what her mother would have said. She saw her sitting there, at the Kapoor dining table, correcting homework. She would look up over her reading glasses and tell Sumi that from where she sat, she could see that Mahima's taunts were stemming from her insecurities, nothing that some genuine appreciation and love could not allay. She was not a mean person; this home was all she had and

Right and Wrong

she wasn't convinced Sumi deserved a share of it, not yet at least, and she would like to see Sumi earn it, just like Mahima had.

Sumi tried. But invariably, Mahima said things that made Sumi say things that she did not intend to.

One afternoon, a few days after Sumi had made the laddoos, Mahima was doling out snacks in serving bowls in preparation for tea with her friends and humming: "Janeman Janeman Tere Do Nayan". She sang well. Early in the mornings, Sumi heard Mahima hum the azaan, matching the muezzin note for note. In the evenings, her melodious singing reminded Sumi of songs that she had watched with Gyan on *Chitrahaar* in the hostel common room on the rare evenings that they were allowed to watch television.

"You sing so beautifully, bhabhi," Sumi said.

"I learned for twelve years," she replied. "When I got married, people in my town were happy. They said now other singers stood a chance of winning the Nightingale Award."

"Do you still sing?" Sumi asked.

"In the kitchen," Mahima said with a sigh. "Lataji has always been my favourite singer."

"But this one is sung by Asha, no?"

"No, don't be silly! It's Lataji."

"No, seriously."

Mahima shook her head confidently, signalling the end to the discussion.

"I have the cassette; we can check," Sumi persisted.

"Okay, bring it." Mahima replied, up for the challenge.

The two sisters had ruled the world of background singing in Hindi films for the last four decades, and were showing no signs of relinquishing. If Lata's voice was silk, Asha's was velvet. If Lata dazzled the listeners by taking them to impossible heights with her vocal chords, Asha lured them into dark, secret spaces in between notes. Both were goddesses of melody in their own right, but there was simply no confusing the two. Sumi ran back to her room and checked the cassette. The satisfaction of being right and the joy of holding a piece of data in her hand flushed through her body. She took it back to the kitchen and showed it to Mahima. Mahima's severe face turned red and she dismissed her mistake with a bewildered laugh. Her tongue almost stuck out in admission of her mistake, but not quite, still staying within the confines of her teeth.

"But look, 'Na Jan Kyun' is by Lataji. That's a better song, much harder to sing." She hummed the opening lines to demonstrate.

Sumi had noticed many times the smoothness with which Mahima vacillated between these two faces. By default, she was confident on her stand, be it her choice in saris, recipes, rituals or politics. The confidence did not always have roots in real experience or knowledge. It was a gamble she made. When she was right, it further entrenched her position of authority. When she was proved wrong, she conceded defeat and quickly jumped over to the other side. If it was a genuine mistake, she would shrug her shoulders incredulously in wonder, inviting others to wonder with her, how she, Mahima, could have possibly been wrong. If it was her bluff that had been called, she laughed a guilty laugh and changed the subject to other things, as if the matter being discussed was trivial in the first place, so it mattered little if she was wrong.

The alacrity with which she swerved from being absolutely certain about something to accepting the opposite view was nothing short of a magician's trick. It created the impression that she was always either fiercely right or blithely cheerful.

To Sumi, this was a sacrilege of the due process of debate. She vented to Dev at night from across the bolster. Dev nodded knowingly as Sumi recounted the argument she had had with Mahima.

"But nothing makes a dent on her. Even when I showed it to her on the cassette cover, she just brushed it off as a minor detail."

"She is like that. She wants to have the last word. Don't take her too seriously," he said.

"It's not about her but the facts."

"She's not perfect, but she has a good heart. She knows the house inside out. This theft, she takes it personally, that's why she makes such a big deal out of it. Takes care of the family and manages the house subtly, so that it takes some pressure off Mummy, but not the glory."

Sumi thought Mahima was anything but subtle. "You think so?" she asked.

"That is what she tries to do. She told me so herself."

※

A week later, as if on cue, Mahima's dire prophecy about more things going missing came true. The next thing to go was the ivory elephant that owned pride of place in the showcase. It was on a late afternoon when Sumi came into the hall with tea that she noticed a blank square staring at her from the centre of the showcase. She half expected to see it resting on the divan, sweeping its fallen stones closer with its trunk, so that she wouldn't sit on them. She would apologise for having forgotten about the cushion, it would dismiss the apology, wrap its trunk around her and gently pull her down to sit next to it and sip her tea.

"Where is the elephant?" she asked, addressing no one in particular.

Mahima and Mrs Kapoor followed her gaze and then looked at each other.

"It was there in the morning. I dusted it myself," Sumi went on.

It was another item that Mahima had brought with her. She had selected it herself, from a shop in the jewellers' market. It had cost upwards of twenty thousand rupees, and that was six years ago.

Mahima shook her head, "This is too much. Your cleaning will be the end of all of us."

The room was suffocatingly hot. A scheduled power cut was going on. The cooler was off and so Mahima could peer through the slits. Pushpa was finishing putting the clothes up for drying. Chhotu was handing her the garments one by one. Mahima walked swiftly to the kitchen and found Pushpa's bag behind the door where she always hung it. Rummaging through it, she found two rotis in a polythene bag, a coin purse with a twisting lock mechanism with twenty rupees and some coins and an open pack of Parle-G biscuits. She ordered Pushpa to stay back that afternoon, and they all went through the house with a fine-tooth comb again. This time, Mahima suggested that they go through everyone's bedrooms too. She tried to make it look fair. Sumi was passing by Mahima's bedroom door when Mahima called out from the dining area, "Why don't you go through my bedroom? Who knows, maybe the boys have been playing with it." While Sumi was in the middle of it, Mahima announced that she would search Sumi's so that they could be done with it quickly. The insinuation of this was not lost on anyone. By an unspoken code of deference, the elder couple's room was exempted from the search. But the elephant was not found.

Mahima walked around with a cloud of outrage about her. Only when Mrs Bansal and Maya came over for tea that afternoon did she step out of it a little. They went through the sequence of events in detail. Maya still did not consider Pushpa as a possible suspect; she would not have the nerve to do something like this twice, Maya was certain. Mrs Bansal asked what it was worth. Sumi furnished details about when she had cleaned the showcase and only then realised that she was the last person to have seen it. Sumi caught Mahima shooting shifty glances at both her friends in quick succession.

"Let's go to the police," Mrs Bansal suggested. "Omji should be the one to talk to them. They're unhappy with me because we never responded to their proposal for Neeti," she said, nodding to Maya. Mahima knew the superintendent's family, they were friends of Om's, and the suggestion seemed to perk her up.

Maya said, "Why bother with the police when we have Naina? She is more interested in what is happening in everyone's homes rather than in her books."

And with that, the ladies resumed talking about other things.

"Dhruv stays up all night, but God only knows what he does. He passed physics by the skin of his teeth," Mrs Bansal said.

"Vivek used to study at night too," Mahima said.

"Diamond, that boy. So hard-working and so respectful. I wish Dhruv had learnt a thing or two from him before he left."

"Will he come for the wedding?" Maya asked. "The priest is saying it will be the week after Diwali."

"That's so close! There's so much to be done!" said Mahima.

"The bride is the least interested in what's going on. She doesn't want to meet the boy again, doesn't even want to select her sari. Nalini is lost in her own world as usual. It's Naina who's decided to behave like a member of the family for a change and help. She's talking to the caterers and decorators. Anything that's not to do with books, she's up for it."

"Keep your valuables locked," Mrs Bansal reminded her. "A marriage house is prime target for thefts."

They discussed the same stories every time. Usually, Sumi enjoyed listening to them fret over the fate of their offspring, but that day she could not shake off the feeling of being suspected of a petty theft. She could not even talk to anyone about it. If she told Dev, he would get properly agitated on her behalf and feel obliged to talk to Mahima, who would laugh and explain to him how absurdly wrong he was to even think of something like that. Sumi wondered how her parents would react to such a situation. Baba would challenge them to think of different what-if scenarios. Ma would say that they were missing the most important variable from their equation: a generous helping of love would set everything straight. Gyan would throw the whole thing out of the window, saying how did it matter, didn't she have an application to write?

A few days on, she received a registered post. It was a marked-up copy of her application. She couldn't wait to see what her father had to say. But when she carefully peeled it open, she was surprised to find that it was not his handwriting. Her euphoria gave way to a mild curiosity. The note was from Gyan.

Baba has finally gone to Haridwar with his friends. The oldie gang has been planning this trip for months now. A study trip, they're calling it, for a paper on the behaviour and motivations of theists. I cautioned him that if he steps inside a coal mine, he shouldn't expect to come out all clean. But I suspect he is well aware of that.

I showed your application to Gautam's cousin who got through physics last year. He says there have only been two applications for hardcore quantum in the last six years and not much happens in that department. He suggested to broaden the scope and slip it under electronic systems, better chance of some action there. Can you think of another topic, something in line with what the department is already doing, and align the outcome and benefits of your research to that? Look at the last page. When are you applying? Can you focus on your application instead of trying out stunts with cooking? You'll do us all a favour by getting out of the kitchen. Ma teared up eating your laddoo. I had to finish them.

She imagined him wolfing down three laddoos in quick succession. With Dev out of the consideration set, there were not many people left to speak to. Sumi had an urge to tell Gyan about the things disappearing from this house and the way Mahima had looked at her.

And what are you doing about it? he would ask.

I'm helping her look for the things.

Anyone can do that. Why don't you use that big head of yours and look for the thief instead?

And just how do you suggest I do that?

Isn't it usually the person you suspect the least? What if the drama queen is pinching these things herself to get attention?

For once, thinking of her brother made her smile.

The Call

Mrs Kapoor was a devout follower of Mata Rani, the Mother Goddess. She had two rosaries, one that she kept under her pillow and the other in the mandir. Each had a hundred and eight wooden beads, one for each recitation of the gayatri mantra. It was a discipline of which she did not have much need, for over the years the chant had become a part of her being, the four lines etched into the grooves of her breath, playing in her mind continuously, two lines per breath, two breaths for each chant. Nonetheless, she liked to do it the proper way twice a day, sitting down with the prayer beads between her thumb and forefinger, nudging one bead down with her thumb with every chant.

When anything of significance happened around her, she paid homage to Vaishno Devi, the holy shrine tucked high up in the mountains of Jammu. The sanctum was a low cave consisting of nothing more than three black sacred stones draped in crimson red cloth and decorated with tiaras and garlands of fresh flowers, but every year millions of devotees undertook a ten-hour hike to get a glimpse of Mata Rani. It was said that one had to go

The Call

when the Mother called. Along the way, the devotees sang together to keep each other going:

"*Chalo bulava aaya hai,*
Mata ne bulaya hai."

"Let us go, one and all,
Let us heed the Mother's call."

When the ascent became too steep, or when the next tea stall was too far away, someone from the crowd would shout "*Jai Mata di*" and everyone would repeat, "Hail the Mother" loudly, infused with a fresh burst of energy to take a few more steps. At the shrine, the queue for darshan snaked around the temple building and into the road and crawled slowly, allowing each devotee no more than half a minute of conference with the Mother, before being gently bumped by the person behind or pushed forward not-so-gently by the priest.

Mr Kapoor complained about going to all that trouble in all that cold to see some rocks, but once Mrs Kapoor's mind was made, he was the one who did everything to make it happen. He booked the train tickets to Katra, and once there negotiated with the local pitthoos to select the finest pony for Mrs Kapoor. During the ascent, he chose the best stalls for food and stopped every two hours for a cup of steaming hot chai.

The trips were difficult to predict. They could be pre- or post-facto; they could be to seek blessings or forgiveness. They went when their first son, Om, was born to thank the goddess for blessing them with a healthy child. When Dev was born one year later though, the prospect of trekking up with two babies in the biting cold was too much for even Mrs Kapoor. Vivek came five years later. He was born at seven months and contracted jaundice when he was three days old. They had to keep him in neonatal ICU for five days. As soon as he was forty days old, she announced that it was time to see the Mother. After years of trying to understand the logic of her visits, Mr Kapoor had respectfully given up.

"Only two people can understand your decisions: you and Mata Rani."

"We go when She calls," she replied.

"Far be it for me to try to understand the intricacies of you two. I will come just for the rajma chawal. Sorry to say, but they are better than even yours."

"It is days old, heated over and over again."

"That's it. That's what releases the true flavour of the beans."

Mrs Kapoor knew that underneath all the tomfoolery was a loving and supporting husband. The Mother worked in mysterious ways, sometimes not granting her most desperate wish and, at other times, overwhelming her with such good fortune as she did not think she deserved. So far, the Mother had been kind. Both Om and Dev were settled. They had good jobs and had married suitably. When she was expecting Vivek, she had secretly desired a girl. Now the Mother had blessed her with two daughters-in-law. They could not be more different, but both were perfect matches for her boys. She did worry about Vivek, so far away at college. She worried about his migraines and whether he was getting decent food in the hostel. Mr Kapoor often teased her for not being a fair mother.

"You worry about Vivek, Dev makes you proud, but it is Om that you have a soft corner for."

"Rubbish. A mother takes care of all her children. She doesn't play favourites."

Although she dismissed him, in her heart she knew he was right. Dev was sensible and hard-working. He got a job in a pharma company right after his BSc, but still he enrolled in evening classes and completed his MSc. He was now a manager in the same company. He earned seven thousand and dutifully deposited five in her account every month. His life was set. Om, although the elder one, was always up to something new. He was not one for books but had a good head for money. He had dropped out of college after the first year, and somehow managed to get a government job with the State Water and Sanitation Department. The job itself did not pay well, but he said no one ever got rich on a salary. He became an agent for the Life Insurance Corporation and sold policies to the entire neighbourhood. His ambitions went further than that though. Money was in real estate, he said. He came up with a plan to pool money with two friends and buy a plot of land on the outskirts of the city. It was a little over two thousand square feet. A highway was being constructed and the value was expected to double, if not more, in the next five years. The seller needed money urgently and was letting it go at a discount at fifty rupees per square foot.

Mr Kapoor had not been in favour of this investment.

"Construction is filthy business. It runs on black money. This is no place for honest, hard-earned money like ours."

But Om was convinced that he had an eye for this kind of thing and went ahead with it. He told them that he had paid one instalment but could claim it back with interest anytime. The other two friends would be happy to buy out his share. Mahima was overjoyed. She announced to all and sundry that they were now "landowners". Mr Kapoor was not happy but accepted that it was not his decision. Every few months he called up real estate agents posing as a buyer and asked what the going rate was. Every time he got a stock answer. It was going for a steal right now. If he was interested in something bigger than five hundred square feet, he could even get him a deal at forty rupees per square feet. Once the highway was up, it would be not a paisa less than forty-five, maybe even touch fifty. He relayed these conversations to Om. Om was unperturbed and reassured him. There were many nuances to consider in real estate. His plot was located right next to the construction site and would fetch much more than the other plots in five years.

But five years was still a very long time, and patience was not Om's strength. He started investing in shares. One of his builder friends recommended Associated Cement Companies. He bought twenty shares for four hundred rupees. In six months, they were trading at nine

The Call

hundred. He added ten more and brought home a box of sweets. Mr Kapoor cautioned him again.

"These kinds of returns cannot be real. We don't understand how these things work."

Om heard him out respectfully, but did not listen to the advice. He added more companies to his portfolio. The market was going through a bull run and within one year his investments had not just doubled but tripled. He paid his instalments and bought two air conditioners, one for his room and one for the hall. The latter was rarely used. Mr and Mrs Kapoor said it made the room too cold and froze their joints. They insisted that the temperamental breeze of the cooler was exactly what they needed. Om asked if it was the temperature or the electricity bill that froze them, but did not belabour it.

The prosperity manifested on his person too. His girth expanded in step with his investments. He was diagnosed with high blood pressure. He had to start taking medicines for it and was asked to cut down on salt and sugar.

Mrs Kapoor kept a watchful eye on him. As long as they were together, healthy and happy, she chose not to get involved in the decisions. Land or fixed deposit, sugar or Sweetex, PhD or children were matters of detail. The ultimate reins of their lives were in the hands of the Mother. The good that happened was the Mother's largesse, and the misfortunes were the fruit of our own wrongdoings, conscious or unconscious, remembered or forgotten, from this birth or a previous one. If something untoward happened, she became quiet and thoughtful. She did not dare to attempt to understand the workings of the divine retribution system, but nothing stopped her from introspecting. She mentally ran a finger down a list of wrongs she might have said or done. If she drew a blank, she ran through a list for each member in her family. She was the mother; everything her children did circled back to her.

So, that afternoon, when Sumi ran up to her room with news of Om, Mrs Kapoor took it in quietly. Her heart was beating to the rhythm of the gayatri mantra, two lines per breath, two breaths for each chant.

Om was in hospital. The phone had rung at about 5 p.m. Sumi answered it. It was Alok, Om's colleague from accounts, calling from the private hospital in Civil Lines. Om had complained of heaviness in the chest after lunch. And then he began to sweat. The general manager's secretary had called an ambulance. Sumi cut him short and asked which room number Om was in. Mahima was not at home so Sumi rushed to tell the parents. Both took in the news without panicking. It was decided that Sumi and Mrs Kapoor would go to the hospital. Mr Kapoor was to keep an eye on the twins, track down Mahima and break the news to her gently. Dev would take them to the hospital later in the evening and one of the ladies could return to see to dinner and the boys.

Sumi and Mrs Kapoor took an autorickshaw to the hospital. Mrs Kapoor carried a prayer rosary in her handbag. She sat through the bumpy ride with her right hand inside her bag, her lips moving silently. Neither of them said anything.

The Call

The moment Sumi stepped inside the hospital, memories of her father's heart attack four years ago came flooding back. They quickly made their way to the room Om was in. To their immense relief, Om was sitting upright on the bed, having a heated conversation with Alok about share prices. The room was much better than the government hospital room her father had been in. This one had a single bed, with a sofa and chair for visitors, a television set and even air conditioning. But the air was the same. It smelled of medicines, disinfectants and fear. Seeing them, Alok recounted the details all over again. The doctor was Om's friend's brother and would take good care of him. The ladies thanked him for bringing Om to the hospital and urged him to go home.

Om told the ladies not to worry. It was only for insurance that he got admitted. He was feeling much better already, although his blood pressure was still one fifty over ninety-five.

"I still think it's the lunch. Mahima knows beans give me gas, but she doesn't listen."

Mrs Kapoor shook her head and mumbled, "Just like his father."

"We mustn't take this lightly, Om bhaiyya," Sumi said. "Are you stressed about something?"

"Me?! Haven't you realised by now? I am not the type who gets stressed; I'm the type who gives stress to others," he said, laughing.

Mrs Kapoor asked Sumi if she could get some tea for all of them. It was unusual for her to ask for tea at this hour, but this was no usual day. Sumi figured that Mummyji perhaps wanted to be alone with her son for a while. Sumi did not mind at all. She could do with some fresh air herself. Om said that there was a new vending machine on the ground floor, next to the reception, that he had noticed on the way in that Sumi could go to.

The machine, situated next to Lord Ganesha's statue, boasted of "expresso" coffee, which was half a cup of sweet, milky coffee, topped with another half cup of froth. It served normal tea and masala tea, both of which came out with a layer of froth too. Sumi stood in the queue, but when she saw the pinkish-brown liquid filling the cup of the lady in front of her, she stepped away. Today, more than any other day, Mummyji deserved a proper cup. She followed the signs to the canteen, but it was overflowing with people. She decided to take a stroll and come back in ten minutes. She walked across the lawn and out of the main gate. On the right was a tea vendor's cart, surrounded by people shouting their orders. Sumi went closer. Tea was boiling in a big saucepan that seemed to have never been washed. It was caked with layers of tea in different shades of brown. Black granules stuck to the outside and inside. The man took the orders and poured more water and milk from equally big saucepans and threw handfuls of tea into the already boiling brew, with no apparent method or measurement. But there must have been because the aroma that his tea gave off was just like home. He seemed to seek Sumi out in the crowd and read her thoughts. He

The Call

raised his eyebrows at her. She held up three fingers and waited.

She took the three cups of tea back to the hospital room. She pushed the door with her shoulder and walked in. Mummyji was sitting next to Om bhaiyya on the bed, deep in conversation.

"Come, come. Thank you, thank you," Om said loudly as she entered. Close on her heels came Mahima and Mr Kapoor. Mahima had not waited for Dev to return. She enlisted Mrs Bansal to watch over the boys and rushed to the hospital along with Mr Kapoor in an auto. She had not changed from her home sari, nor had she done her hair.

Sumi placed the three cups on the side table and gave one to Mrs Kapoor. She offered her own to Mr Kapoor, who waved it away, so she offered it to Mahima, who took it gratefully.

"Without sugar for you," she said, handing Om his cup.

"Hain?" he asked, looking bewildered and hurt.

"What else?" Mahima said, for once in support of Sumi.

He took one sip, and the bitter beverage contorted his face into a grimace. "Stuff like this will make even a fit man sick."

Mrs Kapoor took a sip from her cup and looked at Sumi appreciatively.

"Better give me poison," he continued.

"It's a small price to pay for your long and healthy life, Om bhaiyya," Sumi said.

"Long and healthy is all fine, but what is the point if a man cannot eat and drink what he likes."

"If you knew that today was your last day on earth, what would you do? Which cup would you choose?" she asked, pulling out a familiar debate from her memory.

"Depends on whether you Goddess-Mothers are looking or not!" he said, and laughed loudly at his own joke.

"No one is looking," Mahima blurted, bubbling with anger. "What you do when no one is looking is who you truly are."

Sumi saw Mrs Kapoor look at Mahima in fear.

"I don't know which cup, but I do know that if everyone starts thinking like that, it will be very good for my LIC policies!"

"Please, for God's sake, stop thinking about money. You have two little boys at home. Just get better and come home quickly." Mahima burst into tears. Everyone crowded around her to console her.

"Why must all this happen to me?" she muttered between sobs. "First my things go missing, now my husband is in the hospital. What wrong have I done?"

Om assured her that he was fine, everything was fine and that they should all go home and get rest. Anyway, visiting hours would soon be over. Soon, Dev entered the room and they made plans for the next twelve hours. He would sleep on the sofa tonight and meet with the doctor when he came for his morning rounds. Mahima and Mr Kapoor would come back in the morning to relieve him. They said goodbye and the four of them squeezed into one autorickshaw and went home.

Dev came home at around ten the next morning. There

was a 30 per cent block so no need for an angioplasty. But his cholesterol was high. He would need to eat healthy, no fried or sweet things, and start mild exercising. They wanted to keep him in the hospital for the rest of the day, just to monitor.

It took nearly the whole day to settle the bills and insurance and it was evening when Mahima, Mr Kapoor and Om returned home. Mrs Kapoor and Sumi had prepared a light meal for the patient. At the dinner table, Mrs Kapoor said it had been a while since they had been to Vaishno Devi. Everyone readily agreed to go.

"And this time we will go on foot," she added.

"Mild exercise is what the doctor said," Om complained. "First you will feed me rajma chawal, and then make me climb a mountain. If you want me to go back to the hospital, why don't you just say so?"

Entangled

Lalita and Mrs Kapoor spoke regularly. Their conversations lasted a long time. Sumi was surprised to see how two women as different as these two found so much to talk about. Mrs Kapoor ended every conversation with "rest is okay". After considering her father's health, Om's stress, Lalita's unrelenting working hours, Vivek's absence, the searing heat, the unpredictable power cuts and the soaring price of mangoes, Sumi wondered what was this "rest" and how was it okay? Call it hope or delusion, but Mrs Kapoor was not alone in this – all of Shantinagar kissed the end of conversations with this phrase.

Lalita called one evening and spoke at length to Mrs Kapoor about Om's health. She had found a cardiologist in Shantinagar through Professor Diwakar's cardiologist and recommended that they visit him for a second opinion. She spoke to Sumi too. Baba had come back from Haridwar and had now gone on a tour of the big-four pilgrimages. Gyan had been accepted for a doctorate in history at the university. Sumi was pleasantly surprised and asked to speak to him.

"Congratulations!" she said.

"Ya. How's yours going?" he asked.

"Haven't had the time to sit down and make changes."

"Have you thought about research outcomes and benefits?"

"Not yet."

"Do you even want to do it?"

Sumi had not seen this coming. "What do you mean? Of course I do."

"Doesn't seem like it. It's been months and you haven't changed a word in your application." He did not wait for her to respond. "Do you even know why you chose this as your topic? Other than the fact that you happened to find it in a book lying on Baba's desk and you liked the sound of the question. Have you ever thought what is it that really interests you?"

Sumi felt a familiar anger in her chest. Once again, Gyan had managed to irritate her. Once again, he had a point. There was no real reason why she had selected this as her thesis topic. In fact, that was not the topic she had intended to choose at all. She had scribbled it on top of the writing sheet all those months ago for further discussion with Baba. That was before his heart attack, before marriage popped up as a necessary condition, before Dev and Shantinagar. That promised discussion was still waiting to happen. Since no other title raised its hand to claim the spot, the placeholder title sat back, spread out and got comfortable, and since no further discussion had taken place to fine-tune the text, the draft version renamed itself the final version without much change in content.

It was not that she had not tried. In the last five months, she had read a collection of essays by Bohr. It was an old copy of the book with a few pages missing, donated to her school's library by someone. The only other book she had found on quantum physics was Pauli's *General Principles of Quantum Mechanics*. She liked to underline as she read, so she began photocopying the relevant chapters. On her fifth visit to the copier, the boy who manned the machine kindly offered that she leave the book with him overnight, so he could copy the whole thing for her. He said it would save her a couple of trips and offered a bulk discount of thirty paise a page.

The copier boy was right. The world of subatomic particles was mysterious, if not downright magical. The electron was like an unruly child who defied all rules. It was both a wave and a particle. It had the ability to be in different places at the same time, and the most accurate description of its location was a probability curve of all the possible positions it could be in, a superposition. Until one measured it, which was when the probability curve collapsed and the electron committed to one location. Before it was observed, the question about an electron's location was meaningless. As far as quantum physics was concerned, there was no point in talking about things we could not see. These observations, as baffling as they were, were not new. They had been published, contested, established and accepted by the scientist community a few years ago. Einstein himself refused to accept the probabilistic theory. "Are we to believe that if no one is looking at the moon, the moon doesn't exist?" he had famously asked.

But the real fun started when you put two electrons together. Two electrons in the same orbital could not be identical. If one had a positive spin, the other would have to be negative. This too was something Sumi had learned in secondary school as the basis of the periodic table of elements, and everyone accepted it as fact. They learned by heart that electrons with the same spins as other electrons in the same orbital jump to higher shells, and that is how we get the different elements. What they did not tell you in school was that if you changed the spin of one electron, its partner would change too, automatically and instantaneously. Not just that, even if you move them away from each other, across the room, the city, even the world, the separated partners could, somehow, no one knew how, communicate with each other and change spins. Scientists called this entanglement. These findings were so mind-bending that heavyweights like Einstein had dismissed them. He teamed up with two other scientists and wrote a whole paper to challenge these findings. But he could not. These observations were real and here to stay.

Gyan wanted her to enumerate the outcomes and benefits of her proposed research. What was she to say? Einstein at least understood the science enough to dispute it. Where was she to start? If and when these mysteries were cracked, who knew where it would lead science and what it would do for humankind. It might change the way we look at the world and at ourselves.

She did not harbour any delusions of cracking open the mystery on her own. Minds far bigger and brighter than her own had been at it for decades. But if she could put even one piece of the puzzle in the right place, if she could shine light on even one tiny patch, that would be something, wouldn't it? And what about the outcome? Maybe she would get one paper peer-reviewed and published in *Pramana*. It did not sound like much, when you put it like that, but it was, to her. She wanted to know what was going on in the quantum world, and why the entanglement and telepathy broke down in the larger objects, like the pen she was holding, which was made of the very same electrons. She wanted to sit down with Baba after dinner, with her underlined notes and questions. He would not have the answers, she knew. But he would have read extensively and would tell her how the baton of discoveries had passed hands over the years, how like-minded scientists formed camps, who got along with whom and who didn't. He would cook up lame jokes about Einstein and Bohr going to Heisenberg's for tea and not being able to locate his house. Every question would yield three more questions and four more books to devour. What she would not give for that list right at this moment. All she had now was a musty library with a total of two books on the subject, and a grouchy librarian who barked at anyone who roused him to check out books.

Sumi went with Om, Dev and Mr Kapoor to the new cardiologist. They took all the test results and the discharge summary with them. The doctor was a large man and met them like an old friend. Om's cardiologist turned out to be the new doctor's batchmate. He was happy with his line of treatment and prescription. Om told him about all the foods that he was not allowed to eat now. He took out the bottle of Sweetex from his briefcase as proof. The doctor nodded. He told Om that getting better was entirely in his hands. That carrying bottles of Sweetex would, unfortunately, not do the trick. He would have to actually start consuming them in lieu of sugar. Om lowered his eyes like an errant student. Walking, however much of it he was doing, was all right but not enough. Yoga might reduce cholesterol. It would help with the stress too. He asked Sumi how Professor Diwakar was doing. She told him that physically he was back to normal, but the episode had made him see the gods, quite literally. He laughed and said that was not unusual.

"When our bodies remind us of our limited time in this life, we start looking for hopes of immortality in new places."

He did not charge for the first consultation but asked them to come for a review every three months.

The drive back home was a happy one. Everyone liked the doctor. "He knows his job," Dev said.

Mr Kapoor nodded. "Just by looking at you he could tell that you are stressed. There is still time: sell off that useless plot."

Om dismissed it. "I'm not stressed, Daddyji; you are. But I agree, he is a good doctor. I must thank Lalita aunty," he said to Sumi.

"I will tell her," Sumi said.

"In a few years, we will be calling you Dr Sumi too," he said.

Sumi shrugged her shoulders and smiled.

"Don't mind, I've been wanting to ask you this since before you two got married. I am a man of little brains. What is this thing that you want to do a PhD in?"

Sumi wondered how to explain the quantum world to him without making him take a detour to the mental hospital. She looked at Dev. He nodded encouragingly.

"You know atoms?" she asked.

"Yes, yes, of course, who doesn't. Very dangerous," Om said.

It took her a moment to understand. "No, not the bomb. Atoms are very, very small. Everything in the world is made up of them. Quantum physics studies the particles that make these atoms."

The three men listened with rapt attention.

"These particles show some strange behaviour. One electron can be in two places at the same time. And if you have a pair of them, and change one of them, the other one will change automatically even if it is miles away. But this doesn't happen in the larger objects that these electrons make up. Fascinating, isn't it?"

"Oh, but it does. Happens all the time in Shantinagar. You don't need to do a PhD to find the answer to that," said Om. "Something happens in one house, all the other houses get to know about it, like this." He snapped his fingers. "Even faster than your electrons! Right, Dev?"

Dev shook his head and they all chuckled.

Sumi kept thinking about what the doctor had said about her father. She wondered what hope Baba was looking for. He had embarked on a new experiment, one in which he did not seem to need his old assistant. The fly-on-the-wall ethnographer had seen something interesting enough for him to drop his methodology and get off the wall to take a closer look. She wondered how he was navigating the temples, the smoke, smells, tingling bells, nasal-basal chants of mantras, the sweet offerings and sticky floors. She hoped that his observations were shedding light on his hypotheses, one way or another. Whether they led him towards or away from his past beliefs, she hoped that they would bring him peace. She wanted to tell him that it was okay if he changed his spin. She might change hers, or she might not. Maybe he would jump to the next higher shell of understanding. Maybe he would ask her to join him, maybe not. Maybe she would, maybe she wouldn't. Maybe their spins would not complement each other anymore, but he would always be her Baba.

Something Happened

Dhruv listened as the teacher explained surface tension. He had flashes of understanding, a sentence here, a formula there, but as soon as he tried to wrap his mind around the whole thing, it slithered away. He looked at his watch. Twenty more minutes remained of this hide and seek.

All their life, the Bansals had paddled against the currents to make sure that they did not get left behind and had more or less succeeded. By the time Dhruv grew up and looked around him, he was already on the right side of the current and was content to drift wherever it chose to take him. He did what he was asked. He went to school, helped in the shop, watched television, did his homework and managed to pass every year and move to the next class. He did not try for much more. Most parents would take offence at such casualness. Mr and Mrs Bansal, however, secretly revelled in it. On the surface, they were strict with Dhruv and had the usual discussions of engineering versus medical exams and told him to get serious about life but, deep down, they were content. This casualness was their gift to him. A gift that they had slogged for all their lives, so that their son would not have to worry about where the next meal would come from.

Theirs was already the biggest shop in Shantinagar. The wholesalers were like family. He might marry one of their daughters and expand this to an even bigger store, with imported biscuits, Bengay, Nivea tins and maybe even a back-lit board saying "Bansal and Sons". He would have no trouble running such a store; he had grown up helping around in the shop. He knew where each item was stocked and could tell the weight of a bag simply by lifting it. Till then, they were content for him to do what other youngsters were doing.

The coaching centre was a two-bedroom house, each room used for a different subject. About thirty students sat in the main hall for physics. Dhruv always chose a seat that gave him a clear diagonal view of a girl he liked. Three coolers had been working at full blast until the electricity went off. Now the air in the hall was thick with sweat. Students fanned themselves with their notebooks. The teacher, oblivious to his surroundings, scribbled away on the board.

A soap bubble is being blown at the end of a very narrow tube, radius b. Air (density p) moves with velocity v inside the tube and comes to rest inside the bubble. The surface tension of the soap solution is t. The bubble, having grown to radius r, separates from the tube. Find r.

As he turned and faced the class, students averted their eyes. He caught Dhruv looking in the direction of the girl and picked him to answer.

"What do you think, Mr Bansal? Your head is full of soap. Can you find r?"

"Sir, in this heat it would be more useful to find the air that is flowing with velocity v," Dhruv wanted to say, but he kept quiet and looked down at his notebook. The teacher picked on two more boys and when they couldn't answer either, gave the question to them as a challenge for next week.

Neither Dhruv nor his parents harboured any illusions that he was engineer or doctor material. They knew that he was unlikely to make it to a good public college on his own merit, and even if they sent him to a private one, he would languish at the bottom of his class or somewhere in the middle, like he did in school. A bachelor's degree in commerce in City College would be good enough for him. In fact, it would be best for him. Commerce was in their blood, after all. Also, it meant that he would continue living at home with them. If only Naina had shown the way sooner, he wouldn't have to spend his last year of school cracking his head against strange-sounding numericals.

Dhruv was a night owl too. He liked to go into his room after dinner, close the door slightly behind him, switch off the tubelight and study in the small circle of light from his desk lamp. His room had a smattering of books, mostly second-hand. Currently, he was working through Vivek's physics textbook from last year. There was an unspoken understanding between him and his parents that there was no point in buying new books.

They were expensive and it was not like they changed the content much year after year. Nor was covering new books going to change the outcome in any way. As the physics ma'am liked to say, those who had to pass did it with ten-year-old books, and those who didn't, couldn't do it with all the latest ones.

Dhruv started his shift at around 10 p.m. and kept at it till well after midnight. His study lamp made the sultry June nights even hotter, so he moved his table directly under the window. He looked out of his window into the darkness as he pondered over the soap bubble problem. Physics, like most things in the syllabus, bored him stiff. Even on the off-chance that he did manage to arrive at the correct answer, how it would help the person blowing bubbles, he could not see. Nor could he see the point of cracking the exams and getting into an engineering college and wasting four years of his life when the commerce people would be out into the real world in three years, without half the headache. The darkness outside his window did not offer any answers. But he saw that he had company. There was light in a window of the house across the back lane, diagonally to his left. He saw it again the next night, and the night after. It became his point of focus as he dwelled on the questions. It helped him think. It held answers. If he focused on it for long enough, he came up with a way to solve some of the problems. The light was on when he started his night shift, and went off around midnight. He could make out a fuzzy silhouette of someone at the window. He stared into it absent-mindedly every night but did not really think about it until one night, after which point he thought of little else.

It was just another night. He was working out a physics problem in his mind, looking at the light in the window. His pen fell on the floor. As he bent down to get it, he accidentally switched the lamp off and had to switch it back on. He saw the light across the lane go off and come back on too. Not sure what had just transpired, he switched his lamp off and on again. The light followed. His heart thumped. In the boredom-induced stupor, it had not, until that moment, occurred to him that there was a real, living-and-breathing person to whom that silhouette belonged. A person who was now engaging with him. The most confounding part was that this was someone he knew. The house was number seven, Maya aunty's. He knew Nalini was preparing for medical entrance exams. He switched the light off and on one more time, just to make sure that it was not something his mind had imagined to avoid studying. The lights of number seven responded. Part of him told him not to go too far to find out whatever this was, and instead to get back to his studies. But another part of him went ahead and flicked the lamp switch every few minutes. There was a response each time. The excitement was more than he could handle. The peek-a-boo went on till past midnight, until his eyes refused to stay open anymore. He reluctantly decided to call it a night. As soon as he switched his light off, number seven went dark as well.

The next night, Dhruv set up his table with an enthusiasm he hadn't known before. The window across the lane was dark. He switched the tubelight off and his lamp on. The light at number seven came on, went off and came back on in two seconds. Then it stayed on, as if the silhouette had been lying in wait for him. Dhruv went about his reading for the night. When it was just past twelve, he closed his books and turned the light off. Number seven switched off and on, and then switched off again. It followed this pattern every night. Two blinks, one at the start, one at the end, a "hello" and "good night". On the third night, Dhruv responded. He blinked his light at about 10 p.m., and then again at midnight.

The night flower between number three and number seven continued to bloom. Dhruv did not, even for a moment, entertain the possibility that it could be Naina. She was far too hard-boiled for anything like this. He also knew that Nalini, the most beautiful girl he had set eyes upon, spent her days and nights submerged in books.

One afternoon, he was in the market and saw Nalini and Maya walking at a little distance ahead. This was the first time he had seen her since the nocturnal tête-à-têtes began. Both mother and daughter were slim, tall and had long hair. But one could tell Nalini apart by her hunched shoulders and stooped neck. She walked with hurried steps as if she did not want to be here. She was oblivious to the havoc her presence was leaving behind, not noticing the boys hovering around her hoping for their lovelorn stares to be rewarded by even a casual glance from the object of their desire. Maya, on the other hand, walked with ease, swaying a little with each step, sashaying her plait gently from one hip to another. She scanned the faces in the market and made easy conversation. Dhruv wondered if she noticed all those boys gawking at her daughter. Until last week, he too used to be one of those expectant boys. But today was different. Keen to make eye contact, he turned into the alley on the left, sprinted through the next two blocks, turned back into the main road and started walking towards them. When he got close, he bobbed his head in greeting to them. Nalini looked through him. If she was trying to keep their nightly dalliance a secret, she was doing an outstanding job. Instead, it was Maya who smiled and asked what he had come to buy. She was making a batch of mathris in the evening and asked whether he would like to come around and collect them, or should she send Naina? He said he would come and collect them himself, quickly stealing a glance at Nalini for any sign of affirmation. She was staring intently at the ground. Her reticence made whatever this was a thousand times bigger. If she had looked at him, acknowledged him in some way, he would have been tickled witless. Their eyes would have met, some notes would have passed, maybe they would have even arranged to meet somewhere, pretending to talk about maths or chemistry, without it becoming a scandal. But her denial made the whole thing real, something much more serious, that needed to be kept a secret. Tantalisations of a kind that he had not known were possible thumped in his chest, made him feel breathless and his body taut. Nothing of this magnitude had ever happened to him. He was desperate to talk to someone or do something, but to who and what? He started walking and kept walking until he reached the qabristaan at the end of Shantinagar. He walked amongst the graves, recounting his story again and again.

The ghosts in the cemetery smiled to each other and heard him out. It was not a new story, they had all heard some version of it or the other. Many of them had lived it; why, some of them were here because of it, but Dhruv didn't need to know all that right now. He paced and mumbled till his breathing was back to normal. They humoured him until the sun came down, after which they yawned, stretched their shadows and gently nudged him out of their world, back into his own.

An Elephant Is Saved

The music teacher in Sumi's school, Hussain Sir, hosted a weekly programme at All India Radio. He was fluent in Hindi, Sanskrit, Urdu, Punjabi and English, could read Arabic and spoke a smattering of French. He could quote *Kumārasambhava* and *Macbeth* in the same breath, was trained in classical Hindustani and sang ghazals and Beatles songs effortlessly. He was always on the lookout for new voices for his show.

Sumi mentioned him to Mahima. She tuned the radio in the kitchen to his channel and, together, they listened to the new singers who came on the show every week. Mahima was not easily impressed. Most of the time, she listened to the first two lines and jerked her head sideways, dismissing the singer as unworthy of any further attention from her. Only in the rarest of cases did she pause whatever she was doing and listen to the whole song. Sumi had to admit that Mahima had a good ear, for these turned out to be veteran singers who had trained for years, sometimes decades.

"You should go, bhabhi, you sing better than most of them," Sumi said to her.

"That's all well and good, but how can I go? Who will manage things here?"

"You manage everything here every day. One day you can do something for yourself. They will figure it out."

"That's not how it works. There's a time and place for everything," she said.

But Sumi could see her struggle with the temptation. Sumi knew that Mahima belonged to a tribe that had been brought up to place family ahead of everything else. Sumi did not agree with these boundaries that Mahima had set for herself. That was putting it mildly. It was a waste of talent. Every individual had the responsibility to achieve their highest potential, or at least try to. Even Lord Krishna said so in *Gita*, in the serial that Mahima watched with such ardour that she prohibited footwear to be worn in the hall while it ran, demanding a military-style attention and silence, just shy of ordering everyone to sit with their hands folded and backs straight, and soak in the wisdom from the Lord Vishnu incarnate. Clearly, he had not done a very effective job of making himself understood. In her mind, Sumi started planning for an evening when she would take Mahima to the radio station. They would order food from Maya. She and Mahima would eat early and go in an autorickshaw at six o'clock. Sumi would wait outside the recording room. She might even take her application along and work on it. There didn't seem to be any time to do it in the house anyway. Om would pick them up at eight. They would have a little snack at home, Mahima surrounded by everyone, as she gave a blow-by-blow account of her first performance on radio, taking care not to mention Sumi more than was absolutely necessary. Sumi didn't mind as long as Mahima sang. It was not going to be easy. She would have to start the convincing process now and let it stew in Mahima's head for some time, until she got used to the idea and started thinking of it as her own. That was the only way of getting her to act on it. It was a process Sumi was ruefully familiar with.

Lately she was bothered by a thought that all she had done in her life was don her father's strong-headedness as her own. She had gone with it long enough, until it became hers, not all that different from Mahima. And now that her father's life was taking him on a different path, she was left stranded and confused, like a shadow without its body.

The one person who seemed to know her mind was Naina. She often spoke of her to Dev. He liked her too. "She is like a little sister I never had," he said. "Although she behaves more like a brother."

"I know! Boys are scared of her. I've seen them avoid her on the streets," Sumi replied. "But I wish she hadn't taken commerce."

"Why? Do you also think like everyone that anything other than an engineer or doctor is a waste?"

"No! No! I'm not talking about prestige and all that. More like a linear programming problem. You have a set of resources; how do you get the maximum benefit out of them?"

"Isn't that what every parent thinks in their simple, non-mathematical thoughts?"

When Dev spoke, he looked at the clock on the wall in front or at the elephants on the bolster. As far as he could, he avoided looking at her. But his Adam's apple bobbed as he spoke, jumping to attract her attention, inviting her to look at it.

One evening, Naina came to deliver biryani for dinner. It was a delicacy everyone loved, most of all Om. Maya made it with extra salt and no saffron, just the way Om liked it. As they all sat at the table, he lifted the lid of the bowl and inhaled the aroma. Sumi pictured the cloud of fragrance of clove, cardamom, cumin and coriander rise up his nose and go to his head, pulling his eyes shut on the way. He rubbed his hands in anticipation of indulging his taste buds. Mahima brought a separate tray of food, of things that they had had for lunch earlier, for Mr Kapoor.

"Daddyji, you must be the only person within a five-kilometre radius who does not appreciate Maya's food," she said, placing the tray in front of him.

"Why don't you like it?" Sumi asked.

"People are mad about her food," Mahima continued. "She is so overbooked, she stays up all night preparing for the next day."

"People like it because she prepares it the way they like it," Mr Kapoor said.

"Exactly! Isn't it nice of her to go to all that trouble? And not just for us, because I'm her friend, she does it for every single customer."

"That's not cooking, that's cheating."

"Cheating?!"

"Take your Mummyji. She will make a dish the way it should be made."

"There you go, buttering her up again," Mahima teased.

"No, no, no, she does. She puts coriander leaves in dal. Even though she knows well that Vivek hates it, she doesn't stop. Because that is her dish and that is the way she makes it."

Vivek's name popped up in every discussion in the house. Sumi had not seen much of Vivek; he had left two days after their wedding, yet she felt like she knew him well. Later in their room, sitting on their respective sides of the bed, Sumi said to Dev, "He is not physically here, but he is very much here."

"Ya. The youngest child, the most loved."

"And the brightest, I hear?" Sumi said with a smile.

Dev smiled back. "Yes, quite brilliant. Doesn't talk much, doesn't have many friends. Lives in his own world. You know, those mad genius types."

"What happened with the entrance exams then? I keep hearing stories."

"He put so much pressure on himself that he cracked, that's what happened," Dev said. He stared at the elephant, his brows furrowed.

"He flunked his mock tests and then . . ." He pointed to his temple with his finger and rotated it. Sumi shot him a look of reprimand. Vivek sounded too gentle a soul to be talked about in this way. Gyan, on the other hand, would be a totally different matter. Before she could say anything, she saw Dev's hands shaking. Talking about his little brother had upset him. He was not mocking Vivek, he was sad.

"No, I'm serious. Or maybe the other way round. He psyched himself into thinking that he wouldn't do well in the finals and that is exactly what happened."

He picked at the thread that traced the body of the red elephant in a long stitch. The elephant flinched.

"You know what his problem is? He doesn't talk to anyone. No one. When he didn't get through, he simply decided that he will do commerce. Just like that. I remember exactly how he said it. He was so composed. He sat at the table and halfway through dinner, food in his mouth, he dropped the bomb that he did not want to drop a year, that he had filled out the form for BCom at City College."

"What's wrong with that? Just now you were lauding Naina for doing exactly that."

"But Vivek is different. He loves this stuff. He knows more engineering now than the engineers who come out at the other end after four years. He would die in commerce!"

"So, you talked him out of it?

"It took a while. That day we were all so afraid of saying anything that might so much as graze his battered spirit that we mumbled our way through dinner. Later, we all sat together and discussed it." Dev picked so hard that the thread broke. The elephant bunched up in pain.

"Om bhaiyya was more in favour of letting him do what he wanted to. He said these days everyone is doing an MBA anyway, whether your degree is engineering or commerce or journalism, it doesn't matter. I said, what is the point? It is neither the course nor the college that he wants."

Sumi placed her hand on his to make the fidgeting stop.

"We were getting into a bit of a deadlock. And then you know who broke it?"

"Mummyji?"

He clicked his tongue. "Daddyji. He said Vivek needs a change of air. He was the one who suggested private college. The fees were two and a half lakhs. Add lodging, food and other expenses, you're talking four lakhs."

Sumi took a deep breath. On her teacher's salary of seven thousand a month, that would take over four years, if she did not spend a paisa.

"Om bhaiyya was up in arms. He said it wasn't about the money, it was not the right place for Vivek. Only good-for-nothing rich brats went to private colleges, not simple, hard-working boys like him. I still think it was the fees. He did say it was more than I earn in a whole year."

"What about him? How much does he make?"

"No one really knows, you know. He has his fingers in so many things. He made a windfall in the stock market last year. But a big chunk goes into instalments for his plot. He doesn't talk much about it these days. And if you ask, he starts beating around the bush."

An Elephant Is Saved

"Then what happened?"

"Daddyji's mind was made up. We did the maths. He had one and a half lakh worth of fixed deposits that he broke. I took an advance. Om bhaiyya turned some wheels and coughed up his part. But we still had one small hurdle to get over."

Sumi tilted her head, waiting for him to continue. Her hand was still on his, which had finally stopped picking. The elephant pressed against her fingers in gratitude.

"The boy himself. He said no, it is too expensive, how would we manage the fees. Om bhaiyya slapped him on the back and said that it was a loan and that he had to return it to us with interest when he got a job in an MNC. Daddyji finally convinced him. I went to drop him off."

His hand turned face up and held hers. He still did not look at her, but his Adam's apple bobbed slowly. Sumi fought an urge to reach out and feel it.

"You should have seen the drama. Mummy loaded his trunk with a year's ration of sweets, savouries, papad and pickles. Mahima bhabhi lost it at the railway station. She wept as if it was not a boy she was sending to college but a soldier off to Siachen."

Sumi chuckled. It was not at all hard to picture that. Dev laughed too. She intertwined her fingers into his.

"Each one is a weird character here. The mental hospital is not across the highway, it's right here, in this house. Sometimes I wonder if I did the right thing by bringing you here."

"Why did you?"

"I liked you. Long before you even knew me. I'd seen you visit Professor Diwakar in college many times," he said. "Why did *you* say yes to me? That is the question."

"You were the least weird of all the characters I met." Sumi smiled and held his hand tighter.

Cool Winds

The air was beginning to grow heavy. The sun shone a shade less bright, but the heat did not abate. Summer was coming to an end and so were the mangoes. Pickles and chutneys were being made in attempts to cling on to them until they came back next year. In the Kapoor house too, three stone jars of achar and chutney were sunning on the veranda, soaking up the salt, spices and summer.

On days that were particularly hot, Pushpa brought Chhotu along with her. She worked as a part-time maid for three houses in the colony. Most of her work was indoors, unlike that of her husband, who was an ironing-man, working out of a shed at the end of the lane. He had secured a solid wood table from a scrap dealer and bought a coal-fired iron. He stood at the table all day, ironing the clothes of the neighbourhood. Over the years, he had added a makeshift plastic roof overhead and a small table fan. These did little to shield him from the heat, but it was the best he could do for now.

Chhotu, literally "the little one", spent his days with him. He looked small for his six years, but he had the memory of an elephant. While his father glided a heavy iron over the garments with all his strength, Chhotu took each ironed piece and placed it in its right pile and counted. He knew which clothes belonged to whom. Two blue pinafores for Naina didi at number seven, boys' uniform for Dhruv bhaiyya at number two. They owed him seven rupees from the previous day. When Chhotu was with his father, he was at work. When he was with his mother, it was his time off. He liked coming to the Kapoor house the most because he got to play with the twins and because he knew he would get a banana or an apple from Kapoor uncle. He did not mind that Mahima aunty entrusted him with the job of filling the cooler with water.

"If you want to enjoy the cool air, you'll have to earn it," she said.

The cooler had a capacity of fifty litres that lasted for about three hours, not nearly enough to cool the interminable summer afternoons. Pushpa filled it in the morning and evening when the municipality water supply came on. On some days, there were scheduled power cuts in the afternoon. During those hours, she manually dowsed the khus-lined panels with water. If the wind blew at the right angle and at the right speed, the fan turned and threw some cool air into the hall.

When Chhotu was around, he took care of all of this. Once the cooler was full, he too splashed the khus panels with water for faster cooling. He liked playing with water. He loved to place a drop on the back of his hand, sit in the shade and watch it disappear. He could see the drop getting smaller and smaller. Eventually it vanished altogether, but he had never been able to catch the exact moment when the last trace of moisture evaporated from his hand. He either got distracted by something, or someone called for him, or he dozed off, but that final disappearing act managed to elude him every time.

It was on one such hot afternoon that he was playing with a mug of water in their veranda, while Pushpa washed the clothes. There was a scheduled power cut from noon until 4 p.m., so indoors was as oppressive as outdoors. Pushpa squatted near the tap, with a heap of wet clothes and two buckets. One bucket had clean water and the other had used water, pale brown in colour. The clothes lay in a pile next to her. She rubbed each one with a bar of yellow soap, scrubbed it with a plastic brush, dipped it in the first bucket, rinsed and repeated in the second bucket. She pounded the dirt out of them with a wooden, cricket-bat-shaped paddle and piled them in a heap on the other side for one final rinse in fresh water. Chhotu was making patterns on the floor with trickles of soapy water when Luv and Kush came to the veranda to play. They were crazy about cricket and used the paddle as a bat whenever it was free. They had many balls, of all sizes and material, and made do with whatever was available for the wickets. The veranda was too small for a proper game, and they had been instructed to go on the street if they wanted to play cricket, but that day their lane had been usurped for a prayer ceremony organised by the local temple. A large tent had sprung up in front of their gate. A stage was being set and large speakers were being wired for what promised to be a noisy afternoon. With a power cut inside and the prayer outside, the twins felt entitled to a game in the veranda. They hovered around Pushpa, waiting for her to finish. As soon as she was done, the boys took the paddle and started their game. Pushpa commanded them to be careful, without looking back from the line on which she was drying the clothes. The three jars of pickle presented themselves a logical choice for wickets. Kush and Chhotu were good with the bat. Luv had a talent for bowling. Plus, he was left-handed. He would bowl with a long run-up, just like his idol Wasim Akram, even though his arm wouldn't fully straighten. His batting was average, like Akram's, and for that he got bullied by Kush. It was his turn to bat first. Chhotu bowled and Kush kept the wickets. Luv was intent not to let the other two bat today. He chalked up one run on the first ball, a boundary on the second and two runs on the third ball. His stars seemed to shine today. On the fourth ball, he attempted to heave the ball out of the house for a sixer. The ball, however, took an edge, and Kush leaped in the air and caught it. Luv's dream of a long stay at the wicket was over. It was Kush's turn to bat. Angry and hot, Luv took his position for bowling with the longest run-up ever. With one forceful, elegant swing of his arm, he clean-bowled his brother. The ball smashed the middle jar into pieces and cracked the adjacent one.

Cool Winds

Pushpa heard the noise. Her face turned white. She ran to them and smacked Chhotu on the back so hard his eyes teared up. He didn't say anything. She went inside and fetched Sumi. When they came back to the veranda, Luv and Kush were licking the pickle off the floor, while Chhotu was standing in the shade, tears trickling down his tanned cheeks. The twins stood up and examined their toes. Sumi asked what happened. Pushpa was distraught. She pushed Chhotu in Sumi's direction and ordered him to apologise. Chhotu stood there quietly, staring at Sumi's feet. Pushpa kept saying "forgive him" over and over. The twins too looked terrified, fearing the worst from their mother when she came to know about the accident.

Sumi could tell by the twins' lack of finger-pointing that they were behind this. Chhotu was either too scared or too polite to say so, but there was a reason he was not apologising. She put her hand on Chhotu's head.

"It's okay. They are just children; these things happen," she said to Pushpa.

To the boys she said, "I will talk to Mummy about this, but you have to help clean it up."

Pushpa touched Sumi's feet in gratitude. They threw away the two jars and swept the floor with water and soap.

After a few weeks of use, the khus shrank and bunched up in places, leaving gaps in the panels for hot air to pass through unchecked and uncooled. When the cooler was off, there was a clear line of sight through the blades of the fan, slits of the panel and the gaps. Peeping through from the correct angle offered a clear view of the veranda.

Mahima had just woken up from a hot and sweaty siesta. She had planned to go to the discourse in the lane, but her clammy nap had left her more tired than she had been before.

She had felt quite tired earlier. Not in the physical sense, but more generally, tired with everything and everyone. Something was happening around her, something she was not able to put her finger on. Everything, no matter how big or small, seemed harder. Take this afternoon nap. There was no electricity, the loudspeakers on the road were blaring, competing with the very generators that powered them, and there was a commotion in the veranda. She went into the hall and stood in front of the cooler. Although it was off, sometimes a wave of loo coming from the right direction could waft through the wet khus and get cooled on its way inside the living room. She peered through the slits to see what the noise was all about. She could not hear much, the priest had started clearing his throat on the mic, when she saw Pushpa touch Sumi's feet. A wave of feeling swelled inside her. It was not anger. Anger was not a stranger to Mahima. It often barged in without knocking, like an old friend, looked around, straightened whatever or whoever needed straightening, and went away without much fanfaronade. People around her knew it well too, and accepted it, even feared it a little, which was quite all right by her. But this was something different. This had been festering inside her for some time, a nameless, formless shadow of a visitor lurking in the hallways of her thoughts, looking for a dark, empty nook to put its bags and settle down. At this point, dark, empty nooks were many. It was all very well for Sumi to be friendly to Pushpa. She was not the one who had to supervise Pushpa's work, inspect the corners for dust and check the plates for oil stains. In the six years that Pushpa had worked for Mahima, they had never indulged in unnecessary banter, let alone touch. That was the way it had to be. But trust Sumi to not know this, just as she did not know to not start eating before the menfolk, or not to walk into the hall with slippers on when they watched *Mahabharat* on television, or anything practical for that matter. What was the point of knowing names of singers when she could not sing one line in tune. Mahima could have made a career out of singing, but she gave up her job as a music teacher when she got married. A woman's job was to look after her family. It looked easy but it wasn't. It was an entire life's work. Look at Maya, raising three daughters on her own. It was true that Bhaskar sent her money, but it was Maya who had to feed them, send them to school and college and, now, organise Neeti's wedding.

Sumi, on the other hand, had more degrees than she could keep track of, but rather than putting them to any use for the family, all she cared about was collecting more. But Dev was smitten; Mahima could tell by the way he looked at her. Mummyji and Daddyji were too nice to tell her that no good ever came of girls reading too much. Mahima was not going to be the one to tell her either. Sumi would have to learn the hard way. But all this was beside the point. She was not jealous of Sumi. What she was feeling was a kind of helplessness. Things were not moving forward. One put in a certain amount of sweat and love into one's life, pushed hard enough and expected, at some point, life to kick-start, to run on its own steam for some of the way. Like this cooler. Once it was filled with water, it was expected to suck the heat from the air and send a cool breeze in. But lately, the Almighty seemed to be rationing her power supply. Someone had cast an evil eye on her and her family. It all started with Vivek going away.

Technically he was her youngest brother-in-law, but she knew, and he knew, that it was much more than that. Vivek was the first friend she had made in this house. When she was a new bride in the Kapoor house, busy making food and chai and first impressions, Vivek, a boy of twelve then, was the only one who had asked her how she liked her chai and had made it for her. He was the one who had asked her about her life pre-marriage, discovered her talent for singing, organised a "show" for the family and "presented" his new talent to everyone. It didn't matter that now she was the elder daughter-in-law, with two sons of her own and more responsibilities than even Mummyji. Soon, Vivek would marry and make a life of his own, but that didn't matter either. He would always remain her first friend in this family.

He should never have left. Things started going awry the day he left. To be precise, it started the day he did poorly in his mock tests, which was the day after the prayer for Dev's wedding.

All that loud noise had given Vivek a migraine. With due respect to the priests, the bad singing had given her a headache too. If it were not on her head to host a hundred people, she would have shown them a thing or two about how to serenade the gods. Vivek had his last mock exam the next day. Of course he did not get a good score. She told him it was only because he was unwell and that he would do well in finals, but the poor boy lost his nerve. He was so badly shaken that he messed up his finals and did not even get into the regional college. But he took this on the chin. It was as if he knew this would happen and had already made the back-up plan. He said he would apply for BCom in City College. If you asked her, it was not a bad plan. He would stay at home where she and Mummyji could look after him. Om had been on her side on this. Vivek was the top of his class and was sure to get into engineering in the state college on his second attempt. But Daddyji got it in his head from somewhere that he should be sent away to private college and Dev concurred. Together, they convinced Om and sent Vivek to a college at the other end of the country.

Now Daddyji was getting sore fingers dialling his

hostel telephone number every evening. Vivek's hostel had one telephone for all two hundred and forty students. It was always busy, particularly in the evenings, when rates halved, and all families tried to call and hear their sons' voices. Chances of getting through were higher during late mornings and afternoons, but those were also the times when no one answered. So, every evening around dinner time, Daddyji dialled the hostel number. Occasionally, someone would answer, ask who it was for, holler Vivek's name across the corridors. The general rule was to shout three times and wait for a minute before hanging up. Once in a blue moon, Vivek came to the phone. When that happened, everyone at home forgot all about dinner and waited for their turn at the phone. Mr Kapoor would ask if Vivek was okay, and then pass the receiver to Mrs Kapoor. Mrs Kapoor and Mahima enquired about his migraines and the hostel food, Om asked about his studies, Dev asked if he had made any girlfriends yet, and Luv and Kush fought over the receiver. On days that they managed to speak to him, they all missed him even more.

Om had not been himself since Vivek had left. He joked around with everyone as usual, but when he was alone, Mahima could tell that he was preoccupied. Previously, he used to tell her exactly how he was funding instalments for the plot. He used to show her the newspaper, and together they tracked the prices of the shares he owned. Not anymore. Now she had to look them up herself. She wanted to help Maya with Neeti's wedding. Everyone in the neighbourhood would bring presents, five hundred here, eleven hundred there. But she and Maya were more than neighbours, they were sisters. Others would hand over envelopes to the bride at the reception. She wanted to give no less than five thousand, and she would give it to Maya, before the ceremonies, when it was actually needed. Om, of course, found it excessive.

"I didn't give such a big gift to my own brother!" were his exact words. That was beside the point and just as it should be. What she needed to know was whether they had enough, and what she saw did not look good. The prices of their stocks were going down. She read about someone called the Big Bull who had created a scam and crashed the market.

"What exactly did he do?" she asked Om one evening.

"There's no need for you to worry," he said. "These things keep going up and down."

"Why will I worry? On the contrary, I want to know how he did it."

"By not entertaining so many questions," Om said, irritated.

When Daddyji asked about ACC crashing, he said not to worry, he'd sold it in time.

"Then how will you pay instalments for the plot?" Daddyji asked.

"Leave it to me," was all he said. He was more irritable these days, especially if the questions came from Daddyji, who was still trying to convince him to get out of it.

"Better to face reality and cut losses now, than go on investing with false hope," Daddyji said.

"I agree," Mahima said. "It is eating away your peace of mind."

"You all talk as if I'm doing all this for myself," Om snapped. "It's for everyone, for the whole family. I know what I'm doing and I will manage it, trust me."

"It's not you alone. Everyone is in this with you. Mahima, your mummy, everyone. It's not worth it," Daddyji insisted. But Om did not listen.

And now he was officially a heart patient. Mahima was most thankful to the gods that it was not more serious than it was. She had gone to the temple the day he was discharged from the hospital. But once the relief and gratitude had done their rounds, annoyance raised its hand. Om's poor health sullied her report card. There was no doubt that she was a good cook and it was not really an exaggeration that her desserts were better even than Maya's. Maya said so herself. It had to be his constant snacking in office that had led to the cholesterol and blood pressure. Everyone else at home was doing just fine. Now she kept a bottle of Sweetex in his briefcase, for the rounds of tea he had in office, and sent fruits in addition to lunch. The containers came back clean every evening. A bit too clean. Still, she reminded him every morning before he left for work to not eat outside. But she knew her words fell on deaf ears. And not just with Om. Lately, she had begun to feel that no one listened to her. Take all those things disappearing. It had happened twice, and twice she had barked herself hoarse, looking for the lost items and the thief. Yes, everyone helped look, but by the next day, they seemed to not care. Even Mummyji, strangely, did not seem to care. Mahima was the only one who kept looking everywhere. And when she narrowed down the list of suspects to Pushpa, she was seen as the bad person. Everyone seemed more concerned about Pushpa than the thefts. But what else was there to do? They had had no visitors on both those days. It was either Pushpa or someone from inside the house. What they did not realise was that when they went up in arms defending Pushpa, they were basically indicting themselves.

The other day she had questioned Pushpa about a missing ladle. She made her look through all the shelves and cupboards in the kitchen, the dining area and even the crockery showcase.

"If you cannot take care of the things in this house, there's no need for you to come from tomorrow."

Pushpa was livid. "You are right. I don't need to listen to this after years of working here." She took her bag and walked out of the house.

This is what you got if you spoiled these people, Mahima thought. They started answering back. Pushpa did not come to work the next day. Mahima had to call the other houses and ask casually, inter alia, whether she had shown up at theirs and, of course, she had, punctual to a fault. Mahima and Mummyji somehow got through the day without her. In the afternoon, Daddyji walked over to Pushpa's husband's ironing shed. Mahima did not know what he said to him, but the next day, Pushpa rang the doorbell at her usual time, and resumed her work without even so much as a namaste to Mahima. After mopping the rooms, she came to the kitchen where Mahima was preparing lunch with Mummyji and handed her the missing ladle.

"It was inside one of the boys' school shoes."

"Shoes?" Mahima screeched. "These boys are mad and they will drive me mad one day. God knows what they will hide next."

"Or before," Pushpa said.

Before Mahima could understand what Pushpa meant, she had walked away.

After Mahima had given a sizeable piece of her mind to the boys for hiding kitchen things in shoes, Daddyji sat down with her.

"Mahima beta, all this is not Pushpa's doing. Leave the poor woman alone."

"How can you know that, Daddyji?"

"Even her six-year-old boy returns change, be it five rupees or one. These are honest people."

"Then where are the things going? Is the house swallowing them up? Or do you also think my Luv and Kush are thieves?"

"She has been serving us since before she was married," Mrs Kapoor added. "Never misses work, is never late, doesn't cut corners in her work."

"I agree, she is not our thief, bhabhi," Sumi said.

"So what, Mummyji? When bad times strike, honesty

Cool Winds

is the first thing to go. You all are too kind for your own good."

Although she did not acknowledge it to them, Mahima did concede one thing, if only to herself. She could not say with certainty that Pushpa was the thief, but she had no doubt that she was the best cleaner in the neighbourhood. If she didn't come, Mahima would be left with a large house to manage more or less on her own and she would not have anyone else to blame. So she bit her tongue and let Pushpa do her work.

Before dinner, Mummyji came to her room and told her what had really happened in the veranda in the afternoon. She had checked the story with Sumi and Pushpa, and then with Chhotu, Luv and Kush. She had spent a good hour with the twins discussing the wrongs that had transpired. In their view of the world, the loss of pickles ranked the highest, particularly the sweet chutney, followed by not owning up to their mistake. Letting the blame fall on Chhotu was par for the course. It had taken some talking on Mummyji's part to reverse the order in their minds, and further persuading them to come out and speak the truth to their mother. Mummyji asked Mahima not to scold them when they did so.

"We don't want to punish them for doing the right thing, do we?"

Listening to their account made Mahima angrier still. Not being able to shout at them made a constriction around her stomach. Mummyji was right, of course. So was Pushpa, so was Sumi. Yet, things were going wrong.

And the fact that no one else seemed to worry worried her even more. She suggested more than once that they should report the thefts to the police. But no one took it seriously. No one took *her* seriously. That was it. That was what had been bubbling inside her for some time, not just a few days or weeks, more like a few months. She was not one to name names, but it all started with Dev's wedding. Well, this was her house and those were her things. If no one listened to her, she would simply have to speak louder.

At dinner, she asked Om, again, to speak to his inspector friend. Mummyji protested, saying that would be a bit too much. Om asked what was the point, the incidents were a few days old now; what could the police do? Mahima was not going to take no for an answer, but before she could respond, Mr Kapoor shushed them. He had managed to get Vivek on the phone. Having spent hours dialling, he made the shortest conversation of all. He thrust the receiver into Mummyji's hand and sat down to eat. As Mummyji spoke to Vivek, her face broke into a smile. She turned to the table and announced that he was coming home for Diwali. Everyone got up from their seats and crowded around the phone, waiting for their turn. A happy mayhem of questions and instructions ensued.

"Book tickets now. Shatabdi is cheaper. Don't forget to chain your suitcase under your seat."

"I'll come to the station to pick you up."

"Don't eat too much on the journey; we will keep breakfast ready."

"Don't starve on the journey."

"Don't finish all the chai in the country on your way."

Diwali was three months away, but the happy news lit up everyone's spirits, including Mahima's. Finally, something good was happening. Maybe the Almighty had merely been testing her patience. She was glad she hadn't let herself fail.

Worse Things Than Death

Naina started tutoring two eighth-standard girls. The scandal of someone with ninety-two percent choosing commerce had rocked Shantinagar for a few days, but the tremors were short-lived. The more people talked about it, the more they began to doubt themselves. Who were they fooling, thinking their children would get through engineering or medical colleges? Candidates outnumbered the seats by a few hundred times. If Naina was choosing commerce, there must be something to it. The awe that surrounded her rubbed on to the commerce section.

The girls she tutored had no interest in studying and would much rather watch over-choreographed, bust-heaving movie songs that ran on a loop on cable television. Their parents had no sway over them and engaged Naina as an escalation. The girls were more interested in knowing whether Tiwari Sir left poems for D'Souza Ma'am in Hindi or English, if the couple in biology had really kissed in the new library and whether Naina would go to a girls' college or co-ed. Naina did not mind the questions as long as she received her hundred rupees every month. She dangled bits of juicy information and got them to complete their homework. She could see that the world around her was changing rapidly. This younger lot was different. They were more confident and did not think twice about speaking their mind. When she had gone against the norm and opted for commerce, the entire neighbourhood had convulsed in fits of frenzy. But for these people, shaking the norm was the norm. Their skirts were an inch higher, many of them smoked and two of them were even rumoured to have lost their virginity. They were only three years younger, but already a generation ahead. Naina kept her eyes open and soaked it all in. There was little that happened around her that she did not know, and littler yet that had the capacity to affect her. Or so she thought.

The girls were studying insects and butterflies in biology. As a practical, they had been tasked to determine what kind of fruits butterflies were partial to. Between the two of them, they had put together pieces of orange, apple, grape and a sad, post-monsoon variety of mango that no one even knew the correct name for. They made nectar out of sugar and water, and sprinkled it over the fruit. By the time Naina parked her cycle and walked up to them, they had caught a butterfly. They showed it to her. Its wings were dark brown on the edges, that turned a lighter, yellower shade towards the middle, and then a surprising blue close to its body. The outer bottom corner had two small orange circles, one slightly bigger than the other, with smaller black circles inside, like two eyes on the same side of a face. The girls held it gently, opened its wings to analyse it from the inside, stroked its hairy feet and passed it to each other.

"She likes apple," the first girl said.

"Put it on the grape, let's see if she likes it," the second one suggested.

"Enough! Now let it go," Naina said.

"But we need three for our project," the first girl said. "We only have one so far, and it's the same kind."

She opened her biology textbook to the chapter titled "Insects and butterflies". On that page, along with dried petals of rose, lay a butterfly just like the one in the second girl's hand. Its wings were as thin and smooth as the rose petals, and under its body there was a brown stain on the paper. Naina looked at the page and then at the girls in disbelief.

"What have you done?"

"What?"

"You killed it. What is wrong with you two?"

"What is wrong with you?" the girl shot back. "This is science, this is what we do. Is it too much for your tiny commerce brain?"

Naina turned to the girl holding the butterfly. With clenched teeth, she gripped the girl's wrist. She held it so tight that her hand went limp and her fingers loosened. With her other hand, Naina opened the girl's fingers and let the butterfly go. Then she snatched the textbook from the first girl, put it in her cycle basket and rode away. Angry tears streamed down her cheeks and nose. It was not what they had said. She had more brains than their entire class put together and she did not have to prove it to anybody. It was their casual cruelty that had shocked her. She rode all the way to the qabristaan, parked her bicycle and slumped near the grave lined with marigold bushes. She opened the textbook, and it automatically opened to the page with the dead butterfly. The rose petals had dried and turned a dull brown, pale against the glowing brown, orange and blue wings of the butterfly. Two odd-sized orange eyes stared directly into Naina's. She sobbed uncontrollably. Normally she took pride in not letting anything affect her, but those eyes had found the tears in her heart. Not only was she distraught, she was surprised at being distraught.

As if sensing her grief, Sheru came and sat next to her.

"How can someone be so cruel?" she asked.

The dog looked at her with his yellow-brown eyes. The same eyes she had seen behind the bush by the river, when he was so little he couldn't even chew. He was bigger now. He hung around Chhotu's father's shed in the day and went home with them for the night. Whenever he saw Naina, he came over.

The ghosts watched her from the trees. "There are worse things than death," they whispered, "but she doesn't need to know that right now." But their susurrations swayed the branches and caused a breeze, carrying their words to Naina's ears.

She heard them. She wiped her nose on the sleeve of her T-shirt. She put Sheru in her basket and rode to the butcher's shop. She got some scraps of meat and fed him by hand. They walked around aimlessly for some time and then she went back home. She saw four pairs of slippers at the door. Sumi must've come too, which was unusual.

Naina didn't know much about her yet, except that her mother had asked Sumi to talk her out of choosing commerce. Maybe that's why she had come. The ladies were having tea in the living room. With less than two months to the wedding, these gatherings had turned into planning committees. They were talking about invitations.

"Are you going to invite him?" Mahima was asking.

There was a hush when Naina entered. She nodded namaste to them and took off her shoes.

"How many guests in all?" Mrs Bansal asked.

"One fifty, give or take," Maya said.

"That's a big wedding to host."

"Maya can do anything," Mahima beamed at her friend.

Naina took a handful of pakoras and sat next to Mrs Kapoor.

"If only the bride would cooperate. But she wants to work till the day before the wedding. Who will try on the dresses?" Maya said.

"Nalini can, they're the same size. So can you, for that matter."

"True. If you look from far, you can't tell who is the mother and who is the daughter," Mrs Bansal said.

"Such good-looking girls. Nalini's lashes are so long it's a wonder they don't tangle when she blinks!" Mahima said. "I can't keep my eyes off her. God save her from evil eyes."

"This one is no less," Mrs Kapoor said affectionately, putting her arm around Naina. "If only she would keep her hair long and dress like a girl."

"I don't understand these girls," Maya said. "Neeti is behaving like it's someone else's marriage. No excitement, no joy . . ."

The rue in her voice was palpable. In her mother's view of the world, all three of them were doing a disservice to their looks, their age and the permission that comes with it, to look around and to be looked at. Her mother, whose social situation wanted to take away that permission, begrudged her daughters, who insisted on squandering their gift away.

"Every little thing," Maya was saying. "Next she'll ask me to take the pheras with the groom."

"I'm sure you wouldn't mind," Naina said.

This was a bit too much, even coming from Naina. The ladies were shocked into silence. Sumi looked at Naina. Not with judgement, but intrigue.

"Okay, young lady, that's enough. What is it?" Maya said. "What is wrong with the world today?"

Naina brought out the book and showed them what the two girls had done. They passed the book around.

"Children do these things. Who all will you burn your blood for?" Mrs Kapoor said, stroking her back.

"My niece killed a bird once," Mrs Bansal added helpfully. "This blue jay had wandered into their living room. She wanted to catch it, but it was a high ceiling and she couldn't reach it. It's like a mansion, their house. She got so angry she turned the fan on. Deliberately. It took us two hours to clean up all the blood."

"So much beauty," Maya said, looking at the butterfly. "It is hard to let go of something this beautiful."

"Ya, you would know," Naina said, shaking her head in disgust and snatching the book from Maya.

"It was a beautiful sofa, light blue velvet. Still has splotches of brown," Mrs Bansal went on.

Naina went to her spot at the back of the house and opened the book. A creature so beautiful deserved a better death. She heard footsteps. Sumi walked over and sat next to her. Naina braced for a lecture on the mediocrity of picking commerce.

"I'm sorry about the butterfly," Sumi said.

"Ma sent you to talk me out of commerce, didn't she?"

"She did ask me to speak to you," Sumi replied, but said nothing further about it. They sat in silence for a while.

"It's cruel, what those girls did. But for every cruel person, there's also someone strong and kind like you."

Sumi stroked the butterfly's wing.

"How are you settling in?" Naina asked, staring at the kitchen window of the Kapoor house.

Sumi followed her gaze. "I'm still finding my feet."

"Don't try too hard. This quagmire will suck you in,"

Naina said bitterly. "It quietly feeds on your dreams and joys and spits out a façade of peace and quiet on the outside."

Sumi took this in. She didn't seem rattled by her words. She didn't question or contradict Naina, she didn't try to justify her marrying and coming to Shantinagar, nor did she pass judgement on Naina's shortcut to commerce. Instead she nodded, seeming to understand entirely and exactly what Naina was saying.

"Thank you," she said. "We all make the choices we need to make. I needed to come to Shantinagar to give wings to my dreams and you need to fly away to get to yours."

Neither of them could bear to set those beautiful wings on fire. They dug a hole in the marigold pot, gently laid the butterfly and covered it with soil. Sumi went back in. Naina stayed back, sitting there, looking at her muddy hands and the specks of shimmering blue powder on her fingers.

Time and Distance

Travelling had always been a source of wonder to Vivek. As a child, when they went to visit his grandmother, he looked forward to the train journey. He could look endlessly at the dried-up rivers, the trees whizzing by, the many cows and the occasional monkey. He used to collect everyone's empty kulhads, the earthen teacups, place them at the edge of his open window and count seconds until the wind whisked each one away. Inside grandmother's house, he was struck by how little the house changed, year after year. The back toilet in her house, the one that no one but he used, was illuminated by a lone, dull light bulb. There was a cobweb that ran from the bulb to the ceiling. It stayed there for three years. When it was finally cleaned away, Vivek felt as if a member of the family had been cleared out. With every year, as he grew from a little boy to a young man, his grandmother's house shrunk a little, but the black-and-white pictures in her living room, the dusty bedsheets and the chipped teacups stayed in their places, untouched by the passing years. Going back to familiar places, cobwebs and all, was like stepping into the past.

He was on a train again now, going home for Diwali. The eighteen-hour train journey would get him home early the next morning. He stowed his bag under the seat and settled into the window seat of the lower berth. Passengers of the middle and upper seats too sat with him. They would return to their respective berths after dinner. Until a few weeks ago, Vivek had been torn between going home and not. He missed his family. They missed him too. But the memories of his last few months were still raw. He'd avoided the first opportunity to go home, saying his break was only five days long. But that excuse was not available this time as college was closed for two weeks. When he told them the news on the phone, he could hear their joy travel across the length of the country, trickle through the telephone into his ears and straight into his heart.

He made as little conversation with his fellow passengers as he could, which was not inconsiderable, given the litany of well-meaning questions that were pressed on him. Where was home, when was the last time he had gone, had he locked his suitcase, how was college, was it true that the hostel served the same dal every day of the week, could he use his engineering skills to crack the number lock on their suitcase, who was coming to fetch him at the station, followed by voluntary information about themselves along similar lines. Whenever there was a pause in the conversation, he looked out of the window. It was that moment before dusk when the sun shines very bright, loathe to leave. The trees, farms and cows gleamed with an urgency. At the next station, he bought a kulhad of chai. He sipped it slowly and placed it on the window. A girl of about seven years sat opposite him, watching him keenly. When the earthen cup was whisked away by the wind, she tried to follow it with her eyes as far she could, which was not very far. She smiled at him shyly, and he smiled back. He ordered dinner in the train. The menu was another one of those things that time had not touched. It was the same rice, roti, dal and a dollop of mixed vegetables cooked beyond recognition. He ate a few spoonfuls and left the rest. Out of old habit, he kept the Eclairs toffee that came with the meal in his pocket for later. At the next station, he got down and gave the remainder of his dinner to a beggar. When the train moved, one of his co-passengers climbed up the ladder to the upper berth. The other one asked Vivek to look after his luggage while he went to the bathroom to change. He came back in his nightclothes, made his bed on the middle berth with sheets provided by the train attendants and hoisted himself up the ladder. Vivek then made his own bed. The man on the middle berth leaned over and surveyed the three passengers opposite him and Vivek below, making sure that everyone was comfortable and their suitcases chained. Vivek looked out of the window until his eyes closed and drifted into a peaceful slumber rocked by the rhythmic clickety-clack of the train. He was woken up at six in the morning by loud, nasal calls of "chai, chai, chai" from vendors outside. They were at the second last station. Vivek bought two cups, downed one immediately and kept the other one for later. He waited for the train to start before going to the bathroom. The squatting toilet bowls opened straight on to the stony tracks below. He came back and had the remaining cup. The little girl was awake and waiting to see what he did with the cups. He saw her watching, and placed both cups on the window, one on top of another and they both watched them take flight.

The station had not changed in the last six months: the same coolies striding down the platforms, bullying passengers into letting them carry their luggage; the A. H. Wheeler and Sons bookstalls selling local authors; people sleeping on their luggage waiting for their delayed trains; stray dogs looking for scraps and that cocktail smell of people, old food and old air. Vivek walked out of the station towards the autorickshaw queue. He had managed to convince Dev not to bother coming all the way at this early hour. A little boy, no more than five years old, barefooted, dressed in a dirty T-shirt and shorts, started walking alongside him. A trickle of liquid ran from his nose to his chin, revealing a sliver of clean skin under a layer of dirt. He tapped Vivek's jeans with the back of his tiny hand. The lines of his hands were black with grime.

"What do you want?" Vivek asked.

The boy stared at him. Vivek quickened his pace towards the autorickshaw stand. The little boy matched it. Vivek spotted an empty auto driving by and hailed it. The boy gave him a smack on his thigh with his tiny hands and ran away. Vivek stopped in his tracks. He went after the boy and gave him two rupees and the Eclairs. By this time the auto had moved on and Vivek had to wait for a good fifteen minutes before another one trundled along.

The familiar roads, traffic lights, dogs and cows, and the sight of elderly men doing yoga in the Company Garden, made him uneasy. Till a few months ago, these were roads he had traversed every day. He knew the turns like the back of his hand. As the auto inched closer to home, he heard the morning aarti from the temple, saw the vegetable vendor doing his rounds and noticed the manhole with the missing lid. It was still missing. Chhotu's father ironed in his shed, like he had done six months ago, when Vivek had left for college. There was something cold and uncaring about this sameness. About things that did not change while time ticked onward carrying the world on its back, second by tiny second. Each tick too small to notice. It only became visible when it had gained some quorum. Life could only be seen in terms of months. The minutes were too close to see clearly, each blurring into the previous one and the next. It required some distance to see it clearly, to bring things into focus. But by then, the observer had become a different person. He was not the same boy who had travelled the same road, in a similar auto, six months ago. So, by definition, it was impossible to recollect one's past exactly the way it had happened.

As the auto turned into their lane, Vivek told the

driver to stop near the elderly man pacing by the first gate on the left. Vivek got off the auto and touched Mr Kapoor's feet. Mr Kapoor put his arm on Vivek's back in part blessing, part embrace and part shove towards the door, and told him to go inside while he settled with the auto driver. Inside, Vivek touched the elders' feet and was enveloped in a flurry of hugs, questions and instructions. They all sat around the dining table. Mahima brought him a hot cup of tea. Mr Kapoor, two cups down already, looked at it forlornly and remarked that for the next few days, everyone else in the house would be forgotten. They asked him about his journey, about his room, roommate, classmates and teachers. In turn, he asked what was happening in the house and about Om's blood pressure. Luv and Kush hovered around his bag hopefully. He pulled two toy guns with rubber bullets out of his bag and gave one to each. They squealed in joy and ran away, firing into the air. Mahima brought out a fresh towel and his old kurta pyjama, starched and ironed, for him to freshen up. The bathroom was the same as he had left it. The bottle of Parachute, tubes of Gillette and Colgate were in the same spots that they had always been in. Bars of Lux and Neem floated in a soapy sludge in their soap dishes. By the time he came out, Om, Dev and Sumi had left for work. He went into the kitchen and was sucked into the warm smell of fried cumin and mustard seeds colliding with the pious spirals of jasmine-scented smoke arising from incense sticks from the mandir. The only word that came close to describing that smell was "home". Mahima and Mrs Kapoor were running in unison like two conductors, orchestrating every activity to perfection. A pot of milk was wobbling up to a boil and a pressure cooker was hissing, threatening to spray everyone with a blast of dal-flavoured steam. Then there was the hum of the water pump filling up the terrace tank and the clatter of knives and spatulas, as the ladies cooked. In perfect harmony, there came a loud musical call from the road: the vegetable vendor announcing the arrival of his cart of fresh tomatoes, carrot, radish, cauliflower, ladyfinger, bottle gourd, bitter gourd, green grams, ginger, garlic, potato and onion, stringing his wares in a song and whirling it around the neighbourhood, ushering in the start of a communal domestic dance. Mahima rushed outside and selected some vegetables, as did Mrs Bansal and the other women in the lane. The vendor processed each order, weighed and packed the vegetables in clear plastic bags. He did quick mental maths and they agreed on the bill, never mind two rupees here and there, as long as he threw in a handful of fresh coriander. Mahima placed the bags on the table and Vivek helped her sort them into the ones that went in the fridge and those that did not. He held up the bunch of coriander.

"You are still buying this stuff?" He hated it.

"Of course. What's food without some fresh coriander?" Mrs Kapoor replied on Mahima's behalf, as she went through the purchase.

"Is there any other reason besides torturing us?!"

"Well, if you must hear it again, it adds a fresh flavour that makes you hungry and gets the gastric juices flowing. Good for digestion," she said with a note of finality.

"My gastric juices flow quite well, thank you," he said. "And I don't understand all you women ganging up against that poor man, haggling with him for free coriander. Why does he entertain you all? Why doesn't he just sell it, like the other stuff?"

"Pay for coriander?" Mr Kapoor said. "The poor guy would have a heart attack if these ladies offered him money for it."

"He enjoys it," Mrs Kapoor said. "He makes up for it in the price of other things, we see to that. Don't you worry about him."

"So much drama for something I don't even like."

"You think you don't like it. There's only one way to find out." She smiled and raised her eyebrows in victory.

"Never!"

"But you know the real reason? It is beautiful to look at. As long as I can help it, I will never serve you anything without it. One day you'll have the sense to appreciate it."

"That's what *you* think," he said.

Quibbling about food was another one of the things that did not change.

They spent the next two days cleaning the house, putting up lights and making a rangoli at the gate with coloured powder. Luv and Kush clung to Vivek every waking minute, playing and eating. At night they fell asleep on his lap, watching television, and he slept the entire night sitting on the sofa. He took them to the shops to buy crackers, sparklers and an assortment of sweets. Mahima declared that they would not make sweets at home, citing Om's heart condition. Mr Kapoor voiced out the unfairness of this, but Mahima said if she made sweets, she would not be able to keep Om's hands off them. Everyone knew that the real reason was that she was upset about Om not escalating the thefts to the police and that this was her way of punishing him. The boys lit a few crackers the night before Diwali but kept the majority for the main day. They begged Vivek to stay after Diwali, as they had barely had any time to play with him. When Vivek said he couldn't, they held on to his arms and bawled, until he gave in and said that he'd think about it.

On Diwali evening, as was customary, they donned new clothes and went to visit close friends with a tray full of gifts. It was usually filled with an assortment of sweets and savouries that the ladies had prepared together earlier, crackers for the children and something for the kitchen. Between the three homes, the ladies knew what kind of bowl or tray or glasses were needed in each other's homes and gifted exactly that.

They started with the Bansals. The adults congregated in the living room and Vivek was ushered to go meet Dhruv, who was still in his room. Vivek climbed up the familiar flight of stairs. The same dusty painting of sunrise, or sunset, hung on the wall. The same string of brass bells, alternating with bright green stuffed parrots and purple, yellow and red pompoms, hung from the spindle of every step. He even remembered that the last parrot on it was missing an eye. This stray memory resurfaced unbeckoned and tugged at his mind. He leaned over to check and was greeted by an unseeing parrot.

Dhruv was sorting his bookshelf. The two young men nodded at each other's presence. Although they had known each other all their lives and Vivek was only a year older, him being in college while Dhruv was still in school created a distance that commanded respect. Dhruv stood aside, making room for Vivek to come in.

"What's happening?" Vivek asked, walking over to his study table.

"When did you arrive?" Dhruv asked.

"Day before."

"The first semester must be ending soon?"

"Ya," Vivek said, going through Dhruv's stack of books. He recognised some of his own.

"Be careful with this one," Vivek said, holding up his old copy of Irodov. "Many wrong answers," he said flipping through the pages.

"You covered the whole book?"

"Two times. I marked out those questions with a highlighter. Wasted many nights on them."

"I am stuck on this one," Dhruv said, pointing to a numerical problem:

> *(i) A satellite is moving around the earth in a circular orbit at half the speed of earth's escape velocity. Determine the height of the satellite above the earth's surface.*
>
> *(ii) If the satellite is stopped suddenly and falls freely to the earth, calculate the time it will take to hit the earth.*

Vivek pulled Dhruv's chair and sat. The answer came back to him like breath. He took an open notebook and started writing the solution, while Dhruv stood behind him, watching the answer unfold.

Mrs Bansal called Dhruv from downstairs to give him snacks. He excused himself and went down. Vivek barely noticed. Once he started working out a problem, he was lost to the world. Everyone knew that. When he was done with the first part, he looked out of the window, organising his thoughts for a second. The view from the window, however, stopped him mid-thought. The back window of number seven was lit by a single string of lights that went on and off. He knew, of course, that Dhruv's house shared the same back view as his own. He had been in this room many times. But seeing that window today, in the same place where he had left it six months ago, gave him a jolt.

Dhruv came back with a plate overflowing with food. He followed Vivek's gaze. He had watched the ladies at number seven put up the fairy lights along the back window the day before. He had watched the lights come on after sunset and had continued watching them into late hours of the night. To him, this was no ordinary Diwali lighting. It was an admission of love, out in the open, for everyone to see, yet seen by none other than him, the one they were intended for. The timid pale yellow flashes that had been playing peek-a-boo from a lone lamp in the dead of the night had now blossomed into green, blue and red lights twinkling, first at a steady pace, like the beat of his heart, growing into long flashes, earnest admissions of desire that worked themselves into short bursts of breathless passion ending with a riotous ripple of light, flowing from one end to the other, a fervent wave starting from number seven, crossing the lane to number two and drenching Dhruv. He watched the sequence repeat, his breath rising and abating to the rhythm of the lights. He allowed himself to imagine that the silhouette at number seven was inside his room, that they were together, pulsating to the rhythm of the lights. It took him a moment to come back to the reality that the person in his room right now was Vivek, and he averted his eyes and thoughts from the window as quickly as he could.

But he had not been quick enough. Vivek had seen him looking at the window. He had also seen the fever in Dhruv's eyes. Vivek's stomach churned and he began to feel warm in his ears. He tore off the paper he was writing on and rose to leave.

"Let me work on this and get back to you tomorrow," he said to Dhruv.

"Are you staying for the wedding?"

"No."

"Okay. See you tomorrow."

He scrambled down the stairs, told Mrs Kapoor that he was going to meet some friends and left the house. He walked through the narrow lanes that were lit with diyas and fairy lights. On the road, people were lighting chakris that spun on their small hemispherical bottoms, spewing sparkles in reckless circles. Children lit fountain sparklers and ran back to watch the sparks shoot up high into the trees. Empty glass bottles were being passed around to launch rockets. Vivek dodged all of them and kept walking. Until last year, he had looked forward to Diwali and lit crackers with a vengeance. He knew where to get the brightest sparkler fountain, the loudest bomb, the most powerful rocket. But today, all he wanted to do was to walk away from this celebration. The light from Dhruv's window had ferreted out memories that Vivek had crumpled and stuffed away in deep corners of his being, where no light could enter. Now, they crawled out of exile, squinting the world into focus, blinded by the jubilations. He came to the market area, which was dead today: all shops closed for the evening. Only the paan wallah was still open. The park at the back was quiet too. He walked in and sat on one of the wooden benches, slouching forward, his face resting on his palms. He felt the folded paper in his pocket. He needed no extra time to solve the second question. He knew what happened to bodies that were stopped suddenly and went into free fall and the time they took to hit the earth. The answer, the real answer, the answer that he could not tell Dhruv, was, today. Today, he felt like he had finally hit the ground. The look in Dhruv's eyes had felt surreal. It was like watching himself from the outside. He could see himself in his own room. He could see his study lamp, stacked against the window. He could see himself watching the window across the lane.

The Indecency of Chemistry

It had been less than a year ago, at the night of mata ki chowki. Mrs Kapoor had organised a communal prayer to thank the Mother for finding a good match for Dev. The entire neighbourhood was pouring in to offer prayers and seek blessings for themselves while they were at it. The house was a flurry of activity. Om was in charge of the tent and music system. Vivek had pushed the dining table to the wall to make room for the shrine and devotees. Dev laid out all the mattresses on the floor and covered them in mismatched bedsheets. Mr Kapoor supervised the twins as they decorated the idols in the shrine.

The head priest and his two stooges arrived and began clearing their throats into the microphone. They were the most regarded priests in the town and took this as a licence to sing out of tune.

Jo bhi tere dar pe aye, wo khali haath na jaye,
Sab ke kaam ye karti, sab ke dukh ye harti,
O Mayya sheranwali, bhar de jholi khali.

The Indecency of Chemistry

He, who on your door lands,
Never returns with empty hands,
O my Mother, help me reach my goal,
O Rider of tigers, fill my empty bowl.

No one said it, but everyone sensed Mahima's tetchy mood and stayed clear of her. Vivek knew she took bad singing personally, especially if it came from her own house. To top it, she had not eaten a morsel since morning. She was fasting, to chalk up extra karma points. He went to the kitchen to check on her. She had made a sweet and sticky halwa for prasad and was doling it out in leaf bowls to hand out to everyone after the aarti.

"My head is going to explode," she said, without looking up.

"I'll make tea," Vivek said, putting the saucepan on the burner.

"Before the aarti? And incur the wrath of Mata Rani?"

"Mata Rani got on her tiger and left the moment these jokers took the mic."

She put the ladle down and looked at him. "You are the *only* one with any sense around here. How I wish I could ask these men to move over and show them how a hymn is sung."

"Why don't you?"

"Then who will do all this?" gesturing to the mess in the kitchen. "But no one else seems to care. Come on, let's have that tea."

Vivek brought a stool for her to sit on, made tea and finished filling the bowls. The tea cleared Mahima's headache and mood visibly.

People began arriving. They took off their slippers outside the door and sat cross-legged in front of the shrine, mouthing the lyrics, swaying silently and clapping softly to the rhythm. Children ran amok, entertaining themselves until it was time for prasad. Vivek took his own cup to his room before the main prayer started. He had to prepare for the last mock test, which was the next day. Although he had gone through the syllabus many times over and had not left any old test paper unsolved, he liked to spend time with his books, going through the same things again and again. He enjoyed it. He felt most at home in the orderly world of mathematics, where there were rules, and the rules worked. One plus one would always be two. He enjoyed physics too, which was really maths applied in the real world. Organic chemistry stretched the limits of logic but was still all right. Carbon flirted with the rules, bonded with another carbon atom and turned into something else altogether in shape, size and structure. Still, there was some kind of code of conduct that it seemed to follow. Inorganic chemistry, though, took things too far. The elements flouted rules and behaved as they pleased. His physics ma'am, who did not get along with the chemistry sir, used to say that there are really no rules in chemistry, just those of physics and maths. The periodic table tried to classify the elements, predict them, rein them in, but some of them still managed to slip away. Elements that behaved differently were grouped together and those that were similar were placed blocks apart. Inorganic chemistry was its own thing, not open to reason. There was a wilfulness about it, a disregard for rules that was almost evil. It was not that he was not good at it. He could reproduce the periodic table in his sleep and knew the rules and exceptions by heart. It was just not decent.

Every few minutes he switched his lamp off and back on again. From a window across the street, another lamp blinked twice:

"Still there?"

"Of course."

Silent messages, spoken in light.

Every time he paused studying, he checked if his companion of nights was around. They had kept each other going for the better part of the year now. He knew, just as everyone in Shantinagar knew, that Nalini studied at night. She was the top of the class in biology, as he was in maths. But entrance exams needed as much time and effort as the school syllabus, if not more. It was true that they were a lane apart and could not study together in the sense of consulting each other face-to-face on physics or chemistry problems, but there was great togetherness in simply knowing that they were doing the same thing, at the same time, checking in on each other with a blink of a light. Vivek had even browsed through the biology textbook, just to know what she was reading. He knew she liked 5Stars. He had seen her buy them in the school canteen. He bought one and kept it in his table drawer, in the hope of giving it to her one day. He tried making eye contact with her in school, but she never looked in his direction. Perhaps she didn't want to acknowledge it yet. Perhaps she wanted to focus on the entrance exams. That was fine with Vivek. In fact, he respected her more for it. He was content to follow her lead. It had started a few months ago, tentatively at first, with a few random, uncertain blinks from her. Vivek had, very cautiously, tested that they were indeed intended for him, before reciprocating. He imagined her sitting with a pile of test papers, cracking seemingly difficult problems with simple, elegant solutions. Sometimes, when he was stuck with an exceptionally difficult one, he looked at her window and in a few moments the solution would come to him. It was like she read his mind and sent her working to him across the lane. Each time he cracked a tough one, he sent his over to her. There were times when he wondered if this was for real or just his imagination. But the random blinks had grown into conversations. And the thought-notes that they exchanged were real. His physics scores were nearing 100 per cent and, to his own surprise, he was doing better in inorganic chemistry too. This was more than he could have ever asked. He was lucky to have her affections and was content with her company across the road, at night, in silence. That night, however, the silence was rudely broken by Kush, who came bounding into Vivek's room.

"They are calling you," Kush said.

"For what?" Vivek snapped, angry at the interruption.

"To bring a mattress."

One of the children, in all the excitement, had held out going to the bathroom for too long and ended up soiling the mattress. If it had been water or tea or oil from the diyas, Mahima would have covered it with a thick sheet and carried on. In fact, if it had not happened under so many eyes, she would have dealt with this one similarly, but too many people had seen it happen, so she had no choice but to change the mattress. The problem was that they had used up all of theirs. Naina offered to bring one from her home and asked if Vivek could go with her and so Kush was sent to find him.

"I'm busy, why don't you go?" Vivek said to Kush.

"Naina didi says I'm too small. She asked me to get you."

"Where is it to be brought from?"

"Her house."

That changed the stakes. Nalini did not want to acknowledge him in public, in the day. This would be neither. She might even come back with them for the aarti and prasad.

"Coming."

He blinked his lamp twice, straightened his T-shirt, ran his fingers through his hair, put the 5Star in his pocket and went downstairs to find Naina. They walked over to her house briskly. He did not talk much. He couldn't, his mind was not there. It was soaring above the houses and trees, floating towards the sky like a happy balloon. When they reached her house, Naina asked him to wait outside. She rang the bell and went inside. Vivek couldn't see Nalini. Within minutes, Naina was back, dragging a rolled-up mattress. She had come alone. Vivek was confused. He placed one end of the mattress on his shoulder and Naina did the same with the other end and they started to walk back to his house. The mattress was heavy, but the disappointment of not being able to catch a glimpse of Nalini was heavier.

"Is she not coming to the pooja?" The question slipped out of his mouth, of its own volition, before he could consider the merits or demerits of letting it out. It was a good thing that he was walking ahead and Naina could not see his face.

"No," Naina replied, from behind him. "She's not at home, she has an extra class at the coaching centre."

Vivek was puzzled. "Who opened the door then?"

"Mummy."

That answer, that single word, took some time to descend on him. And when it did, it crushed his world. It did so quietly, no one heard it. It made no sense. His partner of those unspoken conversations, his succour through those solitary nights was not who she was. Nalini had never hidden her feelings for him in school. Because she hadn't had any. She had never looked at him, in the same way that she never looked at any of the many boys who hovered around her like flies. That one word made a little hole in the balloon and let all joy seep out of it. He found it hard to breathe. The mattress became heavier, crushing first his shoulders, then working its way down, rib by rib, till it reached his heart and squeezed the life out of it. Once they were back at his place, he helped lay the mattress on the floor and went up to his room. He locked the door, shut off the lights and lay on his bed. He missed the aarti. Kush came to his room with prasad twice but Vivek did not open the door. Sleep eluded him. He thought of revising for the test but could not bring himself to sit at that desk and face that window again. He switched the tubelight on, brought his books to the bed and read, but his tears wet the pages and the words began to swim into each other. The next morning, he went for his test red-eyed. He tried to focus on the paper. All the questions were familiar to him, as were the answers. But his eyes watered and his hands shook. If he closed his eyes, one lone light went on and off, and he had to open them again. He was not able to write much. When the results were announced, his coaching tutors were shocked. From being at the top of the class he had dropped to the twentieth centile. He was determined not to repeat this in the final exam, but his mind had convulsed itself in knots, baffled at how it had botched up the most important equation of all. What was the point in labouring at trifling multiple-choice questions until it had worked out this one. He forced himself to read through the nights, but his eyes were not used to the fluorescent white glare of the tubelight. It brought on a migraine that would not go away with any amount of tea or Disprin. He ate little and lost weight. Everyone worried and fussed over him. They thought it was exam stress and he didn't bother refuting it.

Mrs Kapoor took him to the doctor, who prescribed

him sweet, white homeopathic tablets, no tea and dim lighting. Every night, Mr Kapoor came to Vivek's room, sat on the edge of the bed, pressed his feet and asked if it was really the exams or might it perhaps be something else? Almost as if he knew. There were moments when Vivek was tempted to tell him, but he just shook his head. Mr Kapoor said whatever it was, was not worth the stress he was taking. On the day of the exam, Dev drove Vivek to the centre on his bike. Vivek knew all the questions. He started with inorganic chemistry and then worked his way through organic and physics. He wrote down his answers meticulously. He was three quarters of the way through maths when the first bell rang. The effort of cajoling his mind to focus on the paper instead of going back to the events of that night had slowed him down. He had mistimed. Fifteen minutes was not nearly enough to write the remaining twelve answers.

The weeks after the test were a haze. He did not remember very clearly how he passed the days until the results were announced. He did not remember that day very clearly either. Neither did he remember thinking about BCom in the City College. He vaguely remembered filling in the form and the furore it had caused at home. The next clear memory he had was being at the railway station, waiting for the train with Dev, a rolled mattress by his side.

Tonight was the first time he had been able to recollect the incident from a distance at which the little details did not crush his heart. It was the first time that he realised that when he asked Naina the question, he had not specified who he was talking about. He had said "she". He was certain about that because he had never uttered Nalini's name to anyone, not even to himself, even in his thoughts. It was always "she". Because "she" was the only one. He now realised that Naina knew. She had known all along. She had not known how to tell him, so she had taken him along to her house on purpose. She had wanted him to know. She had done it to protect him.

Vivek walked back home with more clarity than he had felt in months. He saw Chhotu, cradling a scared Sheru in his lap, covering his ears, and asked him to get Naina. Chhotu ran, Sheru close on his heels, and returned in a few minutes with Naina. They exchanged nods.

"Commerce, huh?"

"I didn't want to slog."

"You would've cracked it in the first attempt."

"What were my odds if you didn't?"

"My case was different."

"Sorry. It was because of me . . ."

"You were trying to help me."

Naina nodded gratefully. "I wanted to talk to you about it many times, but I could not be sure if it was you at the window or someone else. I thought if I took you home, you would see for yourself and . . . sorry, maybe it wasn't the right way to do it."

They sat in silence. Sheru sat by Naina's feet. All the heartbreak aside, Vivek couldn't figure out why Maya was doing this.

"But why . . ." the words escaped his lips.

Naina shrugged. "It's not the first time. Before this there was an uncle, around the time our father left . . ." Naina's voice trailed off.

Vivek took it in.

"Maybe that's why he left," she continued, talking to herself.

"She does it just for fun?"

"Leaving us to pick up the pieces after her."

"More pieces need picking up now," Vivek said.

She turned to look at Dhruv's house and again at Vivek to confirm that they were thinking of the same person.

"How do you know?" she asked.

Vivek told her what he had seen in Dhruv's bedroom.

"How did you know?" he asked her.

"His window light started blinking a few weeks ago, like yours used to." She paused awkwardly before continuing. "I didn't think she would do it again, so I crossed the back lane to see what he was seeing, and there it was, Ma's window light dancing with his."

"What should we do?"

"I don't know. After what happened with you, I wonder if sometimes it is better not to tell people the truth."

"No, we should."

"Ya. Anyway, it's not like he's going to get through the exams if we don't."

Vivek couldn't help smiling at this.

"Can you not stay longer? I don't think I can do it alone."

Making Sense

The whole house breathed a sigh of relief when Vivek said he'd stay another week. Before long, word spread and the whole street burst into joy. Maya sent a steel container with sweets for him, an assortment of his favourites. Sumi offered to take it to his room.

Sumi liked Vivek. He was a younger Dev. He had the same height, build, the same Adam's apple and bass voice. There was a rawness about him that made her want to protect him, something she had never felt with Gyan. There was a mystery around this quiet, brilliant boy.

His door was pulled close. She knocked and entered. Vivek was reading in his bed. He sat up when he saw Sumi and gave her a shy smile. But when Sumi placed the box of sweets on his table, he recoiled.

"I don't want it," he said with disgust. Sumi was taken aback by his rudeness. She shrugged her shoulders, picked up the container and made her way out of his room.

"Please, sorry. I didn't mean it that way," he said. "Sorry, please sit."

Sumi conceded.

"Sorry, it's just that I can't have any more sweets for

the next few months now," he said, patting his belly. That's how everyone felt after every Diwali, but it didn't quite explain his reaction and Sumi wanted to get to the bottom of whatever it was. She sat on the edge of his bed and looked around his room. It was tidy to a fault. The bed was made, books on his shelf were perfectly lined in descending order of height, and there were no stray clothes on the bed or the floor, unlike Gyan's room, where every conceivable space was taken up by open books and the floor was piled with clothes, fresh and used alike, his trousers collapsed into two circles, the way they had been slipped off. Vivek's suitcase lay open, with neatly folded clothes, toiletries in a plastic bag and textbooks. Sumi picked up a book on the top of the pile. It was *Physical Chemistry* by Sharma and Sharma.

"We had their text for BSc too."

"You teach maths, right?" Vivek asked.

"Yes, high school."

"I got ninety-eight per cent," he said quietly. "Ninety-seven in twelfth."

He wasn't bragging, merely sharing a fact and Sumi received it as such. "I know! Dev can't stop talking about how bright you are. He says you got the brains for all three of you."

"Hardly . . ." he dismissed the compliment.

Underneath the book was a battered and flattened 5Star. "What is this?" Sumi asked.

"Oh, nothing. It's very old."

"Give, I'll throw it away."

Making Sense

"No, it's okay," Vivek said, and grabbed it before she could reach it. He did it with an urgency that startled her yet again. She looked at him, but he avoided eye contact.

"Looks like it is not an ordinary chocolate," she said.

Vivek said nothing.

"Someone gave it to you?"

He shook his head and blushed.

"You got it for someone?"

Silence.

"And they didn't want it?"

Silence.

It looked a few months old.

"Is it someone here?" she asked.

Vivek stared at his feet and blinked hard. He was fighting back tears.

"Let's go for a walk," she said. Before he could say no, she held his arm lightly and led him downstairs. She grabbed her bag from the hall and told Mahima that they were going to buy some last-minute things for the hostel. Mahima added a few things for them to buy on the way.

On the road, out of earshot, Sumi continued to probe. It was not a difficult equation to crack, once all variables were considered. There were not that many girls around them. Nalini was quiet, serious and studious, just like him.

"Is it the pretty girl at number seven?" she asked.

Silence.

"Did she not like you back?"

"I thought she did. But I was wrong."

They passed Chhotu squatting by his father's ironing shed, Sheru sleeping next to him. Sumi called him over, handed him a candy from her bag and continued walking.

Bit by bit, question by question, Sumi got the whole story out of him.

"Maya?" Sumi was shocked and confused. "Are you sure? Why?"

"That's what I've been asking myself for months," Vivek said, exasperated.

"You didn't tell anyone?"

He shook his head.

"When exactly did it happen?"

"Night before the final mock."

"The one you could not write properly?"

He nodded.

"What happened in the exam?"

"It was like someone had pushed me off a cliff. My brain wouldn't work."

Sumi waited for him to go on.

"I don't have a lot of friends, I've never fitted in with people my age. But she's different. When she's around, I feel comfortable. She's like me, she likes books. The few times we've spoken, she gets me, I get her. So when I saw the . . . lights . . . I thought I understood her. And I started talking to her. The first real conversation of my life. You must think I'm crazy."

"Not at all."

"But that's not the worst part." He stopped for breath.

Sumi could guess what was coming.

"Maya aunty knows how I like my brinjal, that I don't like coriander. Before exams she used to send my favourite halwa for good luck. She knows me. She lured me out of my corner and ... for what? What did she want with me? To have fun? Is this all some kind of game for her?"

Sumi was furious. What was Maya doing, flirting with a boy half her age? Did she know that her little game with the lights had dragged Vivek through this roller coaster, that she had not just broken his tender heart but also played with his future and had thrown the entire Kapoor family into a financial tizzy? Or was there a version of this story where she came out looking good? Could she possibly know of Vivek's feelings for Nalini and was this perhaps her way of bringing them closer? As far as Sumi could figure, Maya was either unbelievably naïve or inconceivably conceited. Sumi couldn't decide which.

"I'm such a fool," Vivek went on. "Everyone thinks I'm some kind of genius ..." His voice shook.

"You have been beating yourself up about it all these months," Sumi said quietly.

"... when I'm the biggest idiot there is. Sorry, I didn't mean to be disrespectful to you, earlier, back in my room. But I know her steel containers a bit too well. They fill me with shame."

Sumi brushed this aside.

"You do know that no one cares about your results? All they want is to see you happy."

He nodded.

"There is not a single day that Daddyji doesn't dial your hostel number. Sometimes he even gets through but we can't get hold of you in the hostel."

"I know. I can hear the boys shout my name all the way in my room, but I don't come to the phone. I feel I've let them down."

Sumi imagined Vivek sitting in a darkened hostel room, covering his ears with a pillow to block out the shouts.

"She is doing the same thing with Dhruv now."

Sumi pictured Maya pouring drops of love potion in her halwa and sending it to Dhruv.

"What I don't understand is why?" Vivek continued.

"Who knows?" Sumi replied. "And what does it matter why she did what she did? What matters is what you do about it."

He kept quiet.

"There's no meaning in why things happen. 'Meaning' is not something that sits hidden in the real world, waiting to be found. It is what we, as observers, choose to superimpose on things."

He looked at her blankly. This was not making sense to him.

But she knew what would. "Quantum physics says that there is no objective reality, our universe is a participatory universe. You, the observer, can affect that which is observed. Are you with me?"

He began to nod slowly.

"You can make it whatever you want it to be," she

continued. Even as she said the words, she realised this was the essence of the lines that Gyan had underlined for her in Schrödinger. Her mind conjured up Gyan's face, grinning triumphantly, saying, "Told you."

"Is this your thesis topic?" Vivek asked.

"You know Pauli?"

"Exclusion principle," he replied.

Sumi nodded. "He said that particle physics turns the observer into a god of creation in their microcosm. We have the power to change that which we observe." She was getting breathless. This was the most she had spoken about the topic since she had left her parents' house. "It all depends on you. You need to decide what you are going to do. You can stay stuck in the past, thinking about why someone broke your heart and why you flunked the exam, or you can move on, show everyone that you are every bit the mad genius they think you are."

"That's a long, tenuous leap from your previous argument," Sumi heard Gyan's grinning face say. "I'm impressed that you could make the connection. My big sister is growing up."

She shooed his face away.

"I don't know how they managed the fees," Vivek said.

"That's not for you to worry," Sumi said. "Just focus on your studies and look after yourself. Can you try to do that?"

He nodded.

"And smile once in a while, will you? Or do we have to pay fees for that also?"

A shy smile escaped his lips. He looked like a little boy when he smiled. They bought bars of soap, hair oil, shampoo and toothpaste for Vivek and the things on Mahima's list. He insisted on carrying all the bags. When they crossed Chhotu on their way back, Vivek called him over and handed him the battered 5Star. Chhotu beamed, baring a row of small, off-white teeth, two top ones missing.

Unions and Reunions

The lights Naina had put around the house for Diwali lingered on for the wedding. In fact, number one and two kept their lights on as well. The new dresses that had come out for Diwali stayed out. Neeti wouldn't arrive till a day before the wedding, only just in time to get mehndi, so the ladies went on a series of shopping trips to buy gold, gifts and more saris. Om chose the caterers and Mrs Bansal negotiated with the tent guy. Maya planned the functions and who would be invited to which ones, made guest lists for each ceremony, arranged gifts for the guests and, of course, the menu. Naina made sure everything was done.

By mehndi night, Shantinagar was ready. Strings of marigolds covered the entrance of the multipurpose hall. A temporary stage was set up, covered with red carpet. Fairy lights cascaded from the roof to the ground and climbed back up again, twinkling dimly in the afternoon sun. The contractor blasted romantic hits of Kumar Sanu on a loop on the pretext of testing the speakers. Two red throne-chairs for the couple were stacked in the corner for the next day, currently occupied by pigeons. The room in the corner, usually used for storage, had been cleaned up. They put a big mirror, a few chairs and a label on the door that said "Bridal room". A tired Neeti sat inside, getting a head start on her mehndi. She wore a sleeveless top and a knee-length skirt. Two mehndi wallahs were at work: one applying henna on her hand and the other on her feet.

"Groom's name?" the one decorating her hand asked. He would inscribe it on her hand, hide it in the swirls so well that the groom would have to hold his bride's hand very, very close if he hoped to find it.

Neeti looked least interested. She didn't answer, instead she looked at Naina.

"Leave it," Naina said.

The mehndi wallah continued with his work in silent reproach, gently squirting cool, brown paste into dots and circles that transformed into peacock feathers on the ball of her thumb that spread and filled the palm of her hand, where they grew into creepers that wrapped themselves around each of her fingers from front to back, eventually curling into a graceful paisley on the back of her hand, signing off with a flourish somewhere around her wrist.

"Come," he said to Naina when he was done with both of Neeti's hands.

"Not for me," she said.

"Who's next then?"

The others were yet to arrive. He didn't appreciate being made to wait.

"Why do you call us if no one wants mehndi?" he said and went out to take a smoke break.

Shortly after, everyone arrived. Dhruv peeped into the bridal room, scanned it and looked at Naina questioningly. Naina knew he was looking for Nalini, but he didn't ask and she didn't tell. She went out to find Vivek. She needed both boys in one place, and soon. Tomorrow promised to be a chaotic day. Whatever she needed to do, she would have to do tonight.

The chaos didn't wait for tomorrow, though. This was the first wedding of the next generation, and everyone had dressed up for it, wearing their second-best saris and second-heaviest jewellery, saving the showstoppers for tomorrow. Sheru had a green jacket on, with golden piping around the sleeve holes. Vivek stood at the back, behind everyone, clearly not wanting to be there.

"Where's your mehndi?" Maya asked Naina.

"Later," she said.

"Where's the mehndi wallah?" Mrs Bansal asked.

"I'll go find him," Naina replied.

"Don't worry. Vivek does very nice mehndi," Mahima volunteered.

"Oh, will this boy ever cease to amaze?" Maya said. "I'm getting mine done only by him."

Vivek looked in horror, first at Sumi, then at Naina.

"Let Mummyji go first," Sumi said, coming to his rescue.

"How can the eldest go first? You go." Mrs Kapoor nudged Sumi towards Vivek. Before anyone else could come up with any other bright ideas, Vivek clutched Sumi's hand and led her to the bridal room.

Everyone walked around the tent, inspecting things,

straightening the marigolds, smoothing creases on table covers, and eventually settled down on chairs near the stage. Om brought a plate of paneer tikka "to sample".

"Very soft," he said, passing it around.

"Why are you taking the trouble?" Mrs Bansal said. "Dhruv here will serve."

"I can do. Dhruv, you go get something to moisten our throats," Om said.

"Chai is coming," Maya offered.

"Who's talking about chai!" He winked at Dhruv. Dhruv smiled and nodded in understanding, but did not budge. Om took him to the side, handed him a few notes and gave some instructions.

Just as Dhruv left, Nalini arrived. She wore a crimson salwar kameez. She had no make-up on but had agreed for Maya to buy her contact lenses. Without glasses, her eyes looked even bigger. For once, she'd let her hair loose. It draped her head and back like a veil. The group couldn't take their eyes off her, including Naina.

"What an honour! You finally found time away from your books to grace the occasion," Maya said.

"Lord save you from evil eyes," Mahima circled her hands around Nalini's head and cracked her knuckles on her temple.

"Such a light," Mrs Kapoor said.

"Go get mehndi inside," Maya said to Nalini and Naina. "You're the bride's sisters, try to look the part."

Unions and Reunions

As the two sisters entered the room, Neeti looked towards them and away, like she was expecting someone else. Naina's eyes were on Vivek. She suspected that her mother's antics and his own academic travails aside, his feelings for her middle sister ran true and deep. The moment he saw Nalini, he seemed to soften. He didn't look at her directly, but his face glowed with joy and hope. Naina herself thought these two wouldn't make a bad couple.

Nalini went to her elder sister. Neeti sat with her arms dangling either side of the plastic chair, waiting for the henna to dry. Her legs were almost done. Nalini tucked a strand of hair behind Neeti's ears. Neeti closed her eyes at the gentle touch.

"Headache?" Nalini asked her.

Neeti nodded.

"We need a mattress in here," Nalini said. "She has travelled all morning; she should get some rest."

"I'll get it," Vivek offered.

"Take Dhruv with you," Sumi said.

"He's gone to get something *cold*," Naina said.

"You come then?" Vivek asked her.

"I'm supervising the cooks," she said vaguely, suppressing a smile.

"You both go then," Sumi said to him and Nalini, winking at Naina.

Vivek saw the wink and gulped.

"Let's go," Nalini said to him. "I need to get out of this place already."

"That makes two of you," Naina said.

Vivek gave her a look of reproach.

"You kept your Brilliant sets so well. They look brand new," Nalini said to him.

Vivek nodded.

"But I'm missing one set."

"September?" he asked.

"Yes."

"It's in my room," he said, standing up.

They walked out in long, quick strides.

"Don't forget the mattress, you nerds!" Naina called after them. She and Sumi smiled. For the first time since she had arrived, Neeti smiled too.

The mehndi wallah was back from his break and working on Mahima's hand. Dhruv came back, cradling two big black plastic bags in his arms. He set them in a corner. Om poured small pegs of Old Monk in four glasses and topped them up with Pepsi. He handed them to Mr Kapoor, Mr Bansal and Dhruv. He let Mahima sip from his, then offered it to Mrs Kapoor, who brushed him aside.

Dhruv downed his glass in one gulp.

"That's the way!" Om said, and downed his too.

Two other families arrived. Tonight was a small affair, with only family and close friends, not more than fifty guests.

"What happened to the music?" Mahima asked.

Dev changed the music to dance hits. Om started moving to the beat, dancing to Bachchan's step – left step-left knee bend, right step-right knee bend – with Dhruv following suit. Maya joined them, swaying gracefully. Everyone else looked on, nodding to the music.

Vivek came back with the mattress, Nalini walking next to him with pillows and bedsheets, both deep in conversation. Dhruv saw them going into the room. He got hold of a bottle of rum, Pepsi, glasses and a plate of snacks and followed them in.

Neeti sat on the mattress with her legs bent and back against the wall. Nalini propped her elbows on pillows, so her hennaed hands were suspended in air. Her mehndi was drying already, caking in parts, revealing the deep orange art underneath.

Naina and Nalini took turns feeding their sister. Dhruv made a drink and offered it to Vivek, who shook his head.

"Give it here," Naina said, and took a sip. She put it to Neeti's lips, who took a big gulp and closed her eyes. She looked at Nalini next, but she refused.

"Have it. You'll get good sleep," Dhruv said. He sat on the floor next to her. Vivek sat in a corner, fiddling with a mehndi cone.

"Then, no. I have to study," Nalini said.

Dhruv smiled shyly.

"I'm going to take a nap," Neeti said.

They made space for her to lie down. Bits of dried henna fell on the bedsheet. Nalini brushed them away.

"Let's go out and dance," Dhruv said to Nalini.

Nalini gave him an incredulous look.

"Come on," he begged.

"I don't dance!" she said, annoyed. She took the glass from Naina and took a sip. Her face scrunched in a grimace. Everyone laughed. Dhruv poured himself another drink and gulped it down.

"Okay, let's go for a walk," he said.

"Why would I do that?" she asked.

Naina looked at Vivek, who was looking at Nalini.

"There's no need to pretend here," Dhruv said in a low tone. "I'm here, you're here, everyone's having a good time . . ."

"It's not what you think," Naina said.

"What does he think?" Nalini asked.

"No one will even notice . . ." Dhruv went on.

"What do you mean?"

"What do you mean 'what do you mean'? I know you want to keep it low-key, but this is the perfect time . . ." his voice rose.

"How many has he had?" Naina asked Vivek. He put up three fingers.

Dhruv got to his feet. He was swaying the slightest bit. He pulled Nalini's hand. Vivek leaped from his corner and jerked Dhruv's hand off Nalini.

"She said she doesn't want to," he said firmly.

"You stay out of it. You don't know anything," Dhruv said.

"He knows everything," Naina said.

"What are you guys talking about?" Nalini asked.

"What do you know, huh?" Dhruv yelled, and pushed Vivek and, in doing so, lost his balance, held on to Vivek for support but fell anyway, taking Vivek down with him.

"It's not Nalini at night with the lamp," Naina shouted. "It's Ma."

Dhruv slid off Vivek and blinked at her. Naina helped him sit up and gave him a glass of water.

"What lamp?" Nalini asked.

Naina and Vivek told them everything.

"Wow," Dhruv said.

"And you thought it was me?" Nalini asked.

"Forgive me about earlier," he said. "If I'd known I would never have . . ."

But Nalini wasn't talking to him, she was looking at Vivek. Vivek stared at the floor.

"I wanted to tell you earlier," Naina said to Dhruv, "but didn't know how to. That's why I asked Vivek to stay back, so we could tell you together. Not like this, obviously."

"I'm sorry," Dhruv said to Vivek.

"It's not your fault." Vivek brushed it aside.

"Can't say I'm entirely surprised," Nalini said. "It's just like Ma to make everyone dance around her."

Dhruv rose to his feet and steadied himself.

"What are you going to do?" Naina asked.

"Dance, what else," he said, and went outside.

"We should go out too," Naina said. Nalini didn't move. She was sitting next to Vivek.

"I was hoping to get some mehndi on my hands first," she said, holding out a cone for him.

Naina left them and her sleeping sister and stepped out into the hall. Someone had managed to get the disco lights on. Some ladies were getting their henna done, while everyone else was dancing, including Kapoor uncle and aunty, even Sumi and Dev. Om saw her and pulled her in. The green and red flashing lights and loud music made everything go in slow motion. She saw Maya sashaying her hips, now appearing, now disappearing, like this was her show and everyone was dancing to her music. Dhruv danced next to her, following her every move.

Garden of Ruins

For Neeti's wedding dress, Maya had selected a baby pink sari with silver work. The senior make-up artist was at work adding colour to Neeti's face as she sat in her blouse and petticoat. Her mehndi had turned dark brown during the night. The assistant make-up artist laid out the sari on the sofa and secured the pleats with matching silver safety pins. Naina and Nalini sat there, detangling safety pins from a bunch. Nalini was wearing a purple salwar kameez, a thin necklace and two bangles to mark the special occasion. Naina wore a light-blue salwar kameez and a thick silver bracelet with no make-up.

"Pink is in these days," the make-up artist said, holding a safety pin between her teeth. She offered to do Nalini's hair while she waited for Neeti, but Nalini refused.

"Do you like a high bun or a low bun?" the senior artist asked Neeti.

"Anything," Neeti said.

The girl turned to Nalini for an answer. Nalini turned to Naina, who turned to the assistant.

"I think she'll be more comfortable in a low bun," the assistant said. Everyone nodded, grateful for a decision.

The room was quiet. It had no happy buzz like outside. In here, you couldn't tell a wedding was about to happen in three hours. Naina stood by Neeti and looked at her in the mirror while the make-up artist brushed her hair. Neeti sat still as a mannequin, not interested in what was being done to her face. Or her life. Every once in a while, she looked at the door. Naina could feel her suffocation.

"I'll get something to drink for everyone," Naina said, and stepped outside.

She went out of the hall and walked around to the back where the caterers had set up. Sheru, wearing a pink jacket today, followed her. The chefs were taking a beedi break. When they saw her coming, they stirred to stand up, but she motioned to them to carry on. She sat next to them and asked for one. She didn't particularly enjoy beedis, but going to the paan wallah dressed like this would attract too much attention. They gave her a kebab fresh from the tandoor. She split it with Sheru. It was a cool evening but the heat from the stoves made her perspire. She made sure they had everything they needed, asked them to send a sampler plate and chai for the bride and, on her way back, instructed the contractor to set up a fan for the cooks.

When Neeti's sari was draped, and her hair, make-up and jewellery done, the make-up artist stepped back and assessed her work from all angles and distances. She fussed over the falls of the sari, patted Neeti's hair and straightened her necklace. She pursed her lips. She had done all she could do. She didn't say it aloud, but Naina knew what she was thinking, because she was thinking the same thought. With all the shimmer and glimmer, Neeti did not look like a bride.

"Why don't you go get some snacks," Naina said to both the make-up girls.

With just the three sisters in the room, Naina put her hand on Neeti's shoulder and looked in the mirror. She saw three broken, incomplete individuals, floating around each other, trying to fill each other's brokenness with their own. Even on her wedding day, even as a bride, Neeti looked like she wanted to shrink and disappear. Like a touch-me-not, Naina thought. Nalini came over and held her elder sister's hand too. Nalini was the beautiful lotus that had somehow managed to grow out of this swamp of a family.

"What's going on?" Naina asked Neeti.

Neeti met Naina's gaze in the mirror and shrank deeper.

"Why are you doing this?"

"We haven't been a proper family since you were ten," the bride-to-be replied. "All because of me."

"You're not responsible for any of this," Naina said, anger bubbling inside her.

Neeti's eyes filled with tears. Nalini placed a tissue under them.

"I was in second year. I told Baba I'll start earning in a year, but it wasn't enough. He still left."

Naina swivelled Neeti so she was facing them both.

"It's all my fault."

"We've been broken for longer than we've been whole. But that's not your fault, or hers," she looked at Nalini, "or mine. Everyone did what they wanted to do, you don't owe anyone anything. Do what *you* want, for *yourself*."

"I should never have been born," Neeti said, unleashing tears that no amount of tissue could contain.

Naina hugged her sister tight. She was the keeper of this garden of ruins.

"Do you think he'll come?" Neeti asked, sobbing like a child.

Both the older sisters looked at Naina with hope.

"Ma did invite him," Nalini said. "Bansal aunty convinced her to."

"Of course, she would. To share the expenses," Naina said.

"I'll do this just for a chance to see him again," Neeti said.

"Don't hold your breath," Naina said. She opened the door and shouted for tea.

※

Bhaskar did come. The girls could tell by the knock on the door. Naina opened it. He stood at the doorway, a bag on his shoulder, just like it was month end and he had come bearing gifts, only he was a greyer version of himself and it wasn't the end of a month or a year, more like the end of a childhood. Or three.

Neeti froze in shock. Naina was too angry to let him in. It was Nalini who asked him to come in.

He looked at his daughters one by one, taking in how each had grown in the last six years. He opened his bag and handed Nalini an album of leaf specimens he had collected over the years. Each was glued on a separate page, along with their name, date and location. The opposite page was blank.

"For your sketches," he said. There were more than a hundred pages, some rare ones she had never seen before. Some had paintings underneath them. "This was purple on the underside. The colour began to fade so I made a painting, so you could see."

He turned to Neeti. "You're good at whatever you do. Whatever you touch turns to gold. But you forget to play. This is for you to play," he said, handing her an envelope.

Then he turned to Naina. After six years, Naina was looking at the face she had waited for, pined for, been angry with and then slowly, stealthily, without letting anyone notice, not even herself, most of all herself, pushed into the dark corners of her mind, where even she couldn't see it. Now that face was in front of her, looking at her, looking into her eyes.

He held a sketchbook up to her tentatively, as if to say if she didn't want anything to do with either it or him, he'd understand. But Naina took it.

It was a painting book, with pages and pages of the same scene. The riverbed, two cycles, one man, three girls, trees and birds. With every page, the cycles moved a little further ahead. On most pages, her hair was in his face. She reached the last page and flicked through them again. The cycles moved. From the entrance of the forest, all the way to the river and back home. On these last pages, she was slumped against his chest. He balanced the cycle with one hand, the other held her close to him, her hair in his face. There were at least three hundred pages.

Neeti broke down. He held her in his arms, tears in his own eyes. She bawled like a child, her mascara running down her painted cheeks. Naina and Nalini held hands and let each other cry too.

"If you weren't my daughters, I would ask for your forgiveness. But you are my little dolls, I will not put such a heavy burden on you. Just know, if you can, that there wasn't one day that I did not think of you, talk to each of you, not one night when I did not tell you stories."

"Why did you leave?" Neeti asked through sobs that shook her whole body. "Why didn't you stay with us?"

"I tried, but there wasn't space for me here."

Naina was livid. "Look at us," she yelled. "This one's getting married in three hours, but all she cares about is whether you will come. This one has lost herself in books, looking for you in plants and animals. And you say there was no space for you? Don't you dare lay this on us."

She shook as she spoke. Nalini held her. Neeti looked at her reproachfully.

"No, gudiya, not on you," he said gently. He held out his hands, but did not touch her. Neeti grabbed them. "There was no space for me to be the man I was, to be the father I wanted to be. I had to go away to stay me,

Garden of Ruins

the me who can hold my head high when I say I love my girls."

He nodded to the envelope and said to Neeti, "This also has my address and a key to my house. Your house."

There was chatter outside the door. Maya entered. Husband and wife acknowledged each other like old acquaintances.

"Thank you for sending me the invitation card," he said.

"Of course."

"The arrangements are very well done."

"I had help," she said, looking at Naina.

"How have you been?" he asked.

"Running around; doing all this," she said. Then her eyes landed on Neeti.

"What's this mess?" she asked, horrified. "Where's the make-up artist?"

"It's nothing," Neeti said.

"It's not nothing. You look like a wreck." She picked up the make-up brush in one hand and held Neeti's chin in another.

"I don't want it," Neeti said, jerking her head away.

"What do you mean, you don't want it? What don't you want? It's all very well for you to shrug your way through finding a match, a date, sari, jewellery, your own wedding. What *do* you want?"

Neeti did not answer.

"I am going home to get dressed. By the time I come back, I want to see you looking like a bride," Maya said, and stormed out.

Black Magic

Maya draped her grey chiffon sari in front of the mirror. She didn't pull the pallu tight over the front, instead she let the soft see-through fabric caress her black sleeveless blouse and hover over the neckline. Neither did she bother securing it on her left shoulder with a pin. The gossamer clung helplessly to the rise of her bosom and the dip of her waist. The conceal was more tantalising than the reveal, Maya knew this well.

She had spent the past few months planning every last detail, seeing to all the minutiae for Neeti's wedding: the flowers, tents, invitations cards, guest list, chairs, menu, sweet boxes, gifts, saris and the gold. She had had no doubt that Bhaskar would show up. Amongst the three girls, Neeti was the one he had always been most protective about. He wouldn't miss her wedding for anything. She didn't need his contribution, but she was certain he would shoulder that too. A part of her was even looking forward to seeing him, to see how he had fared after all this while, and for him to see how she had. But not like this!

The girls had flocked to him like starving waifs, unfed

for years. He sat with them, hugging, listening, nodding, like he understood it all, every single thing. They clung to him, hoping he could fill the void. He held them close, wanting to become whole. Seeing him see the slumped mess that Neeti was had filled Maya with an unease. It was a long-forgotten unease, going back twenty years to her own wedding. It was a hazy unease. She couldn't recall the colour of the tent or whether there were marigolds or roses, the time of the day or even which sari she had worn. She had worked hard to forget all that.

She put on a thin eyeliner and just a shimmering nude lipstick. This was Neeti's day and she had no intention of stealing her thunder, although she knew she would. It was not the height of her bun or the arch of her eyebrows. It was the way she carried her head high, the assuredness of her shoulders that elongated her neck, the straightness of her spine upon which her hips curved and fell that turned heads. When people saw her, they let out a gasp. It was a tiny one, sometimes audible, sometimes not, sometimes visible, sometimes not, but it always happened. She could sense it.

Synched to an invisible clock, all three neighbours emerged from their houses at the same time. Mrs Bansal took in a full inventory of Maya's jewellery. She did quick maths, accounting for the real gold chain, the artificial pendant, silver bangles with gold plating, the arm band that snaked around her arm, and said, "All combined it is not more than six thousand, but on you, everything looks royal."

"Because she is our queen," Mahima said, cupping the air around her friend's face, careful not to smudge the foundation. "Put anything on a queen and it will become royal!"

"May the Mother protect you from the evil eye," said Mrs Kapoor, gently patting Maya's bun in blessing.

The men said their namastes and asked if anything needed to be carried to the venue. Bearing the last few gifts and fruit hampers, they proceeded to the multi-purpose hall. At the entrance, they were greeted by a cool, rose-scented mist from the fans. Naina had outdone herself. The red carpet was brushed so clean it looked new; the chairs had crisp white covers; on the stage sat two thrones and shehnai played softly from the speakers. The hall had transformed into a room from some palace.

Maya took it all in, but something was gnawing at her. A waiter came bearing a sample of papdi chaat for her to taste. She waved him away and went to the make-up room to check on the bride.

Bhaskar was sitting next to Neeti, holding a plate of chaat. He acknowledged Maya but his eyes didn't linger on her. If he registered how resplendent she looked, he did not let on. He did not gasp. He never had.

The make-up artist had cleaned up the mascara and kajal and done a round of touch-up. The pink lipstick matched exactly with the sari. The kajal, bindi, nose ring, tikka, necklace, bangles were all as they should have been. The shade of foundation was perfect for her skin. And yet, Neeti looked nothing like a bride. She sat slouched, eyes staring blankly at the floor. She looked tired. But not from the two-hour-long make-up session; she looked tired of life. Seeing this decked-out, disinterested bride opened up the floodgates of memories Maya had buried deep down.

In Neeti, Maya saw her eighteen-year-old self, sitting next to Bhaskar for the rites, taking seven rounds of the sacred fire, promising each other love, loyalty, duty and whatnot. She remembered the heaviness of those steps, not because of the sari, but because of the shame that she carried inside of her, that was growing every minute, taking shape, preparing to come out in the world for all to see. Heavier than the shame was the anger. She was angry with herself that she had not seen this coming.

Maya didn't like surprises. She liked to be in charge of her life. She was the third of six sisters. Her parents barely managed to feed and clothe all of them. The sisters attended school until sixth, while it was free, and then joined their mother in cleaning and cooking in other people's houses. Their father worked as a security guard by night and driver by day for Gupta Saab.

Maya's dreams were bigger than this hand-to-mouth existence. Even as a teenager, Maya knew she was meant for better things. But her family was too busy surviving to indulge her fantasies. They owned one spotty, ten-by-eight-inch mirror on the wall. At night, after everyone had slept, Maya would look at herself in the mirror by candlelight and watch the fire burn in her eyes, the shadows caress her cheekbones and kiss the base of her neck. Darkness was her friend. Magic happened in the dark.

When her oldest sister got married, she moved up in the chain and started accompanying her mother to Gupta Saab's house to clean. It was there that she saw for the first time her magic at work. Their son, Vinod, did a double take when he saw her, like he couldn't believe so much beauty was possible and gaped at her to make sure his eyes were not playing tricks on him. She enjoyed going to their house just to watch him look at her. She stood exactly in the gap of the kitchen door through which he could catch a glimpse of her. Whenever she was there, he felt thirsty frequently and came into the kitchen to get water or ask for tea. When no one was around, his fingers accidentally brushed against hers. He liked paneer. She made it just the way he liked it, with extra garlic and a garnish of fried whole red chillies. He liked them burnt.

"There's magic in your hands," were his first words to her. "You cook very well."

Maya was underwhelmed. This wasn't the compliment she was expecting. She looked at him with an eyebrow raised, unimpressed.

"Is that all?" she asked.

He blushed and went out.

The next time he said, "You have pretty eyes."

She looked straight into his and asked, "Is that all?"

When her second sister got married, she took over the household entirely. Gupta Saab and Memsaab used to go

Black Magic

to the club once a week, leaving Vinod at home, alone and hungry.

One such evening, he said, "Your hair is so long."

Maya slid the pin from her bun and let the black magic unfurl down her back and engulf them both. They tumbled and tossed through its dark alleys. Maya discovered depths of passions and heights of pleasure she did not know existed. After the first time, there was no stopping them. She enjoyed their weekly lovemaking as much as she enjoyed the interlude of six days. She watched with satisfaction as Vinod writhed with desire, looking at her hungrily. She became radiant, unstoppable.

Her parents started receiving matches for her. She would have to get married soon; there were three more after her. When she told Vinod this, he said he couldn't last six days without her. If she married someone else, he would most certainly die. He would talk to his parents the next day.

Days turned into weeks, and while Vinod didn't speak to his parents, Maya's parents received an offer for their fourth daughter and Maya realised she was pregnant.

When she took this happy news to Vinod, she wasn't prepared for what she saw. She saw how quickly burning desire morphed into cold disgust. Her own parents were mortified. How could she bring dishonour to the family? What of her three unmarried sisters? With no one else to turn to, Maya went to Memsaab. Memsaab turned to her son and asked if this was true, if he had indeed made the guard's daughter pregnant.

"You think I will stoop so low and touch this filth?" he said.

After this, everything was a blur. Maya didn't feel the slap on her cheek, only heard the tinnitus it left. She heard "gold-digger", she heard Baba fall at Memsaab's feet and grovel to keep his job. All marriage offers disappeared except one. Someone called Bhaskar, a widower ten years older than her, who didn't think of her as damaged goods, who didn't mind the unborn baby, who said that all babies were made of love.

The baby girl was the spitting image of Maya herself. Every time Maya looked at her, she felt a sickening mix of shame, disgust and pity. Neeti sensed this even as a baby. She recoiled from Maya and turned to Bhaskar for anything she needed. Bhaskar accepted Neeti as his own and loved her for the both of them. He kept all the seven vows and more. He provided well, he did not care for her looks, treated her as an individual instead, with respect. He was a good husband, a good man.

It was only when Naina was a toddler that Maya emerged from this haze and realised that she could never love a man like Bhaskar. She had tried. Nalini and Naina were living proof of that. But she wanted to be loved hungrily. Bhaskar's love wasn't hungry; it was kind and gentle. She needed the world to know her magic, she needed to convince him, convince the world that she wasn't filth, but how could she convince one who didn't consider her to be filth in the first place?

She had been relieved when he finally decided to leave.

It had broken the girls' hearts and fractured their childhood, Maya was fully aware of this, but there hadn't been anything else to do.

Seeing him here after six years, Maya felt herself soften and was surprised by her reaction. He had greyed but, other than that, he looked exactly as he had all those years ago.

She looked around the room.

Naina sat by the window, seething. The smallness of this life stifled her. Maya knew the suffocation well. She also knew Naina would break free the minute she could.

Nalini was untangling Neeti's kaleere that had got knotted up in all the hugging and crying. Nalini was the daughter who perplexed her. Beauty was a gift. Maya wanted to shake Nalini and tell her not to squander her gift. There was so much to enjoy in the real world, outside books. Maya had even tried to show her how it was done. There was that diamond of a boy Vivek, sitting at his window just across the lane, alone and awake, night after night. She knew he liked Nalini, she had seen the way he looked at her, all shy and hopeful. A few blinks of lights, that's all it had taken: some sparks to kindle a little flame. Vivek had caught on and the flame danced on both sides, through the nights and through the lights. So much left unsaid, so much left to imagine, Maya could feel the flush of young naïve love course through her. But Nalini paid no heed and soon Vivek left for college. Thankfully, Dhruv was still here. He was gorgeous in his own way.

And then there was Neeti. Her firstborn. Born of her first love and, really, her only real love. Every subsequent love had been an experiment, a game to see if she could still summon the taste of that first love. Each one had had its own flavour, but none of them came close to the real thing. Somewhere along the line, she decided it was useless to chase the past and had started to savour whatever life put in her way, here and now. In Neeti, she saw herself. She wanted to tell Neeti that life was beautiful, that she was beautiful. She was not filth, she wanted to say.

"Why do you look like someone died?" was what came out of her lips.

Neeti did not answer.

"Answer me. Do you want this marriage or not?"

"Of course she does," Naina said. "She can't wait to experience the thrill of marital bliss we've all had the pleasure of seeing."

"Give your bitterness a break. I'm talking to your sister."

"Do you like the boy, gudiya?" Bhaskar asked.

Neeti did not look up.

"Do you want to settle down, start your own family?" Maya asked.

Silence.

"Why did you say yes? No one pressured you," Maya said.

"Do you want to go back to the hostel and keep working?" Naina asked.

Neeti looked at her and took a long breath. She looked at the room and the hall beyond the room.

"I've been running around like a mad woman buying your saris and jewellery, putting all this together, the baraat is coming in two hours and you sit here looking like a martyr. What is going on in your head? Speak, for God's sake!" Maya was shouting now.

"Why did you say yes if you don't want to get married, gudiya?" Bhaskar asked.

"All the problems in this house are because of me. I didn't want to cause any more trouble," Neeti wailed.

Maya had spent a lifetime picking up pieces of her own mistakes, putting herself back, and here was her daughter, ready to make the exact same ones.

"That's it. I'm calling it off," Maya said.

Everyone looked at her in shock.

"You don't live your life like an apology. This is your life. You decide what you do with it."

Bhaskar's eyes brimmed with admiration. For the first time, Maya saw Naina look at her with respect.

"What will everyone say?" Neeti asked.

"You don't make decisions based on what others will say, not even your own family," Maya hissed. "Have I taught you nothing?"

Death of a Butterfly

Naina watched as Maya and Bhaskar broke the news to the others. Bhaskar asked one of the waiters to get chairs and water for everyone. Maya put her arms around Mahima, explained that there had been a misunderstanding.

"But what about the tent?" Mrs Bansal asked.

"Naina will talk to them," Maya said, looking at Naina.

"And all this food?" Mrs Bansal enquired again.

"Naina will take care of it."

"It's not a good omen to send the priest back without the ceremony," Mrs Bansal said.

Om spoke with the priest and gave him something from his wallet.

"What about the groom?" Mahima asked.

"We will go to them now and make apologies," she said. She looked at Bhaskar as she said this.

"Shall we come with you?" Mrs Kapoor asked, Mr Kapoor by her side.

Maya and Bhaskar accepted their offer gratefully.

Dev, Om and the boys helped get the tent down. Sumi,

Mahima and Mrs Bansal went to make calls and inform the other guests.

Naina managed the caterers, asked them to pack whatever had already been cooked and take back the rest; they'd be paid in full.

The children had a run around the hall, aiming marigolds at each other. The contractor changed the CD to sad songs of Kumar Sanu while he took down the lights and the stage. The throne-chairs were loaded respectfully into the truck, placed on rolls of carpet.

Back in the room, Nalini and Naina helped Neeti take off her jewellery, sari and make-up. She wouldn't eat. They made her swallow a few spoonfuls of rice and took her home. She couldn't sleep. Nalini lay beside her. Naina pressed her feet, massaging her pedicured toes.

Maya and Bhaskar returned late at night. Bhaskar came into their room and the girls insisted on hearing everything, no details spared. The groom's parents had been livid. This was not how these things were done in this society, the groom's father said. They should never have agreed to a girl from a fatherless home, his mother said. She had been uncomfortable with this match from the start. The boy had asked after Neeti, how was she coping with all this, what were her plans now. He seemed relieved, almost. The boy's parents asked if they could speak with Neeti and see if she might change her mind. Maya had stood firm, said sorry, that wouldn't be possible. Bhaskar and Maya apologised to them and their extended family again for dragging them through all this humiliation and inconvenience, but hoped that, as parents, they would understand that they couldn't let their daughter compromise her happiness for the rest of her life. Mrs and Mr Kapoor gave them the gifts that had been bought for them including the gold, enough to cover the expenses they would have incurred and some more for good measure. They blessed the boy and hoped he would find the right match at the right time, asked for their forgiveness again and came back.

Bhaskar stayed back and talked with his daughters. They covered six years in one night. Neeti told him things about her hostel and work that she hadn't told any of them. She had been promoted twice in two years, she was the youngest assistant editor they had ever had, the only woman ever. He told them about the township that he had designed. The centrepiece was a playground which had a blue slide that snaked around the playground like a river. It was surrounded by bushes and trees, some rare varieties. Some trees were shaped like animals.

Neeti finally slept, but not before making Bhaskar promise that he would be there when she woke up. He said he would stay for as long as they wanted and would leave only when they'd tell him to.

Nalini was next to close her eyes. Naina dared sleep to venture near her. She didn't want to miss even a second of this night. She had so much to say, so much to ask. But now that it was only her and Bhaskar in the room, she was afraid to look at him. What if he was tired and needed to sleep? What if he had had enough and wanted to go back? She was scared of what she might see and upset that she was scared. She stared instead at the blanket that covered her sisters.

"Would you like to go for a walk?" Bhaskar asked.

They walked without talking. All the houses were dark. They walked in the dim light of the streetlamps. The light on the main door of the hall was on. There were still things to clear in the morning. They walked to the main market. The paan wallah was still open.

"Gold Flake?" Naina asked Bhaskar. He tilted his head in acceptance.

The paan wallah recognised Bhaskar.

"I tell gudiya it's not good for her, but she doesn't listen," he said, father to father. Bhaskar nodded in gratitude.

They got two sticks and walked back. From a distance, they saw Maya opening the lock of the multipurpose hall. The light of the side room came on. She must be collecting Neeti's things.

"Let's go and help her after this," Naina said, taking a drag.

Bhaskar agreed.

Although the wedding had unravelled in the most embarrassing public fiasco, it had brought the family together. For the first time, they had acted like one unit and saved Neeti from making a foolish decision in the name of duty. Naina had known all along that Neeti was making a compromise, giving up her joy and freedom hoping for acceptance, but she hadn't been able to stop it on her own. She had tried, but it had taken all of them to pull it off.

Neeti was exhausted, true. She would need months to recover from this aborted marriage, as would all of Shantinagar, but that was a small price to pay to get another chance at life.

Although all five of them had been there, Maya was the one who had had the courage to call it off. Naina could delude herself all she liked that she was independent, that she did not need her mother, neither for herself nor for her sisters, but in the end, it was Maya who had pulled Neeti out, not even blinking before casting away months of preparation, effort and expenses, not caring about the scandals and humiliation that would ensue. Naina felt weak. She sat on the side of the road. Bhaskar sat next to her. She leaned her head on his shoulder. He cradled her face in the crook of his elbow.

They were a ruin of a garden no doubt, but a garden nonetheless. It was shrivelled up by distance and time, but today it had felt like there still might be some life left in it. Naina wondered what tomorrow might look like. Perhaps if they stayed together, it might rain, it might soften the parched soil and let something grow? A tiny hope fluttered inside her. She was used to carrying the weight of her incomplete family. She had been carrying it for six years. But this little butterfly of hope was more than she could bear. She sank into her father. He put his arm around her.

Death of a Butterfly

"Close your eyes," he said.

She did. She dropped everything she had been carrying, everything that had happened, that was happening and that might happen. She felt light, for the first time in as long as she could remember. They sat in silence. There were so many questions she had asked him so many times in her head: Did he miss her? Did he wish to come back? Did he hate Maya for pushing him away? Did he wish he had taken them with him? Sitting next to him, hearing his voice, smelling his smell was the answer to all of them.

Footsteps sounded in the distance. Someone had arrived at the hall. Naina peered in the darkness and saw Mrs Bansal and Dhruv. They knocked on the door, and Maya came to open it. From across the street, Naina caught snatches of conversation.

"I said I'll go and check if you need a hand, but Dhruv insisted on coming along," Mrs Bansal said.

They took two large bags to drop at Maya's.

They were barely out of sight before a Bajaj Chetak stopped in front of the hall. It was Suresh from number twenty-five. He had just got engaged.

"I saw the lights on and thought I'd check."

Just as he rode off, one bag balanced between him and the handle of his scooter, Negiji from number fifteen arrived in his Maruti 800. He had been living on Maya's food since his wife passed away four years ago.

"I know how hard it is, managing everything alone."

"I'm almost done," Maya said.

"Then let me drop you home," Negiji said.

Maya came out carrying the last few things. She switched off the light, locked the hall, sat in the car and they drove off in the direction of Maya's home.

"Looks like we are not needed," Naina said.

Bhaskar stared at the road. He didn't say anything. Naina sat up straight. Bhaskar was not needed now, never had been and never would be. This is what he had meant when he said there was no space for him to be the person he wanted to be. He had lived through this. He had left when he couldn't live with it anymore.

After a point, if the earth is too parched, no matter how much you water it, it doesn't soften. It can't. It turns into rock. All the water slides off it. Nothing can grow on a rock.

Naina took a deep breath and closed her eyes. She caressed the butterfly flitting inside her, took in all the colours it had promised, kissed its soft, smooth wings goodbye and, gently, very gently, closed her heart on it.

"You should leave by tomorrow's train," she said to Bhaskar. A shimmering, rainbow-coloured dust stayed on her lips. It tasted bitter.

The Things We See, Part II

The evening before Vivek's departure, the mood in the house was morose. Everyone sat down for his final dinner; it was a meal with all of Vivek's favourite dishes. Mrs Kapoor doled out food on his plate and Mahima poured him a glass of water. The twins sat on either side of him. Like bees sucking as much nectar as possible before their beloved flower closed for the season, Sumi thought. Mahima dished out more dal for the twins than they usually had, but they knew better than to protest today. This was not a good time to lock horns with her.

It was too hard to think of the house without him, so they focused on his upcoming journey instead, and went as far with him as their worries would take them. They spoke in low tones over the clanking of spoons on plates. Everyone, individually, confirmed the train schedule and discussed how many autorickshaws they would need to take him to the station.

The susurration was broken by Mahima.

"Mummyji, where's your bangle?" she asked, with an edge in her voice.

Mrs Kapoor looked at her bare wrists. "I took it off when I went for a bath. I must've left it in the bathroom."

A complete hush fell over the room. Everyone, except Luv and Kush, stopped chewing their food. Mahima asked if anyone had seen the bangle. No one had. No one had even noticed that she was not wearing it.

Mahima pushed her chair back, leaving her food as it was, got up and went to the bathroom to check. It was not there.

Om and Sumi got up too.

"Maybe I took it to my room and kept it somewhere safe. I'm getting forgetful."

"You say anything, Mummyji," Om said. "It must be in your room only."

"I'll go look," Sumi offered.

Seeing her, Dev arose too and then Vivek, automatically followed by Luv and Kush. Mrs Kapoor gestured to Vivek to sit back down.

"You all are worrying unnecessarily. At least let the boy eat his last home-cooked meal in peace. Then we will look together."

Sumi came back saying it was not on Mrs Kapoor's bed or side table. Mahima pursed her lips and did not say any more. She did not ask whether Mummyji had gone for a bath before or after Pushpa left.

"Did any outsiders come home after your bath?" Dev asked.

No one had. Mahima did not need to ask Om to talk to the police.

The Things We See, Part II

"I'm going to call my inspector friend," he said.

Mr Kapoor was about to get up, but Dev told him to keep sitting, just tell him where to look. Mr Kapoor just shook his head. Dev went to check the hall and Vivek took the boys to look in the kitchen.

They turned the house upside down, even took everything out of Vivek's neatly packed suitcase, but found nothing. The food went cold, and the collective sadness turned into collective frustration. They finished dinner half-heartedly and turned in for the night.

The next morning, Mahima made Pushpa search the whole house again. It took over an hour, with the result that Pushpa had not been able to clear the kitchen before she had to go to her next house.

"It can't go on like this," Mahima hissed at Pushpa.

Pushpa had had enough too. "You make up your mind about what you want me to do and tell me tomorrow. I need to go now," she said. She tied a black thread on Vivek's wrist, with strict instructions not to remove it for three months, not even while showering. She had got it from a hakim who specialised in migraines. She told him to come back soon, wished him a safe journey and left.

In the afternoon, Chhotu came to deliver their ironed clothes. Sumi took the pile, paid him and handed him a banana. He dithered for a moment and looked at her, as if to say something, but went away without saying anything.

Sumi felt that afternoon was quieter than usual.

Everyone was trying to rest, not looking forward to the trip to the station. The house was dead silent, when there was a gentle tap on the door. Sumi opened the door and found Naina. She greeted Sumi with a slight nod.

"Can you come outside for two minutes?"

"Sure, what is it?" Sumi said, stepping out and pulling the door behind her. Chhotu was by the gate, with Sheru by his side. Naina gestured Sumi to walk down the lane, away from the house. When the three of them reached a quiet spot, she stopped and turned to Chhotu.

"Tell her," Naina said to him.

Chhotu glanced from Naina to Sumi. He looked scared.

"What is it? Are you all right? Is Pushpa okay?" Sumi asked him.

Chhotu first nodded his head and then shook it.

"What's happening?" Sumi asked Naina.

"Don't be scared," Naina said to Chhotu. "It's Sumi didi. You can tell her."

"I have seen it," he mumbled.

"What have you seen?"

"The elephant."

"What elephant?"

He started to sob and shake his head. Naina signalled to Sumi to go closer to Chhotu. Sumi knelt down and put her arm around him. Between jerky sobs and half sentences, he told her.

He was in the veranda, putting water in the cooler. It

was a hot afternoon and there was no power. He saw Mrs Kapoor get up from the divan, take the elephant from the showcase and go to her room. She returned in a few minutes and lay back down.

"Are you sure it was the elephant that she took?"

He nodded, looking down at his worn rubber slippers.

"When did you see it?"

"That day when Mahima aunty made Amma stay back late and look for it."

"Why did you not tell us before?"

"I was scared."

"And now?"

"Mahima aunty is calling Amma 'thief'. Amma is angry. She doesn't want to go to your house again."

"Pushpa is thinking of leaving the colony," Naina said. "Chhotu doesn't want to go. He came to me earlier today. He didn't know who else to talk to. Likewise, I didn't know who else to tell, so told you."

"You did the right thing," Sumi said. Turning to Chhotu, she said, "Don't worry, no one is going anywhere. Just don't say anything to anyone till I figure this out."

Vivek's train was at 7 p.m. By five thirty, his suitcase was packed and everyone was ready to see him off. Everyone made sure, individually, that he had his tickets, cash, food for the journey, food for the first two days back in hostel, umbrella for the rains and warm clothes for winter. Sumi too made a list of books for him to refer to in his library.

If all seven of them were to go, they would need to get

a third auto. Sumi offered to stay back and keep an eye on the twins. Vivek touched her feet. She hugged him and told him to call home regularly.

As soon as they left, Sumi went to Mummyji's bedroom. The elephant was no small item; she would most certainly find it. She went through her cupboard, groping around under Mummyji's stack of saris. In the far right-hand corner, she found a small coin purse, the size of her palm. Inside was the gold bangle, carefully wrapped in a magenta tissue paper, the kind used by jewellers to wrap small earrings and pendants. Folded along with it were two loan receipts from a jeweller in Bada Bazaar in Azadganj, where Mummyji sometimes went to pay respects at the Bhairon mandir. Fifteen thousand rupees, a loan against a medium-sized ivory elephant studded with semi-precious stones, four thousand rupees for a silver plate with engraving. Sumi took a deep breath. She was relieved that Chhotu was right and that she had been right about Pushpa not being the thief. But she did not know what to make of her discovery. Why was Mummyji stealing things from her own house? What possible reason could there be? How did the moral gatekeeper of the family allow herself to stoop this low?

Now that she had been led to the truth, it made no sense and she did not know what to do with it. She did not want to keep the bangle in her possession as it was too valuable, not to mention dangerous. How would she convince Mahima that she had not taken it in the first place? She wrapped it carefully and placed it back exactly where she had found it. But she kept the receipts with her so that she had something to work with. Maybe she would get a copy made and return the originals. She closed the cupboard, switched the light off and left the room.

The Quantum of Physics

Sumi was torn. Her exhilaration at finding the culprit was weighed down by the humiliation she would bring upon Mummyji if she outed her. But she could not be expected to sit quietly while things kept disappearing from the house and Mahima found no other scapegoat than Pushpa to punish.

Gyan came to see her on his way to a conference. Lalita sent an assortment of sweets and snacks from their local snack shop back home. She sent a light shawl for Mrs Kapoor, and a book of lyrics for Mahima. It had five hundred film songs, listed alphabetically, cross-referenced at the back by the name of the movie, year of release, music director and playback singer. Mahima was pleased. It had some songs that she did not even have cassettes of. She immediately retreated into the kitchen and came out half an hour later with her famous halwa for Gyan. After lunch, Sumi took him to her room.

He settled on her bed, the bolster in his lap. Sumi settled on the other end. From where she sat, she could see the red elephant feeling Gyan's chest, deciding whether it liked him or not.

The Quantum of Physics

"How is it going?" he asked.

Sumi told him about the thefts, about Vivek, about how clean he kept his room, about Chhotu's account and the bangle that she found under Mrs Kapoor's saris.

Gyan let out a soft whistle. "It is always the one you'd least suspect," he said.

"And Mahima bhabhi is making Pushpa's life hell for no fault of hers."

"But why is Aunty doing it? All this belongs to her, why must she steal?"

Sumi spread out her hands in ignorance.

"What will you do?" he asked her.

"I have to tell them, don't I? The truth must come out."

"But what is the truth?"

"What do you mean?"

"Do you know why she did it?"

"What does it matter?"

"What if she has a reason?"

"That will make this right?"

"Who knows. You don't know what you don't know."

"There you go, confusing things unnecessarily."

"And you, looking for blacks and whites. The truth is usually somewhere in between. Isn't that what your particle physics says about the world?"

"Why did I even tell you all this?" Sumi said, a familiar irritation rising in her.

"Has to be something in the family," he went on.

"What do you mean?" Sumi asked, getting more and more annoyed.

"When one electron changes spin, the other also changes, doesn't it? Maybe it is someone in the family."

"You mean there are two people involved? From inside this family? There you go, talking about things you know nothing about. These are simple, straightforward people who quibble all day over small things but would die for one another in a heartbeat. They are not petty thieves." Sumi was breathless. "Leave it, no point talking about this with you. Just don't mention it to anyone, not even Ma, okay?"

Gyan nodded in agreement. "Leave all this. Have you submitted your application?"

Sumi shook her head. "There's no time. Some drama or the other keeps happening."

"Stop making excuses. Fifteenth is the deadline. If you can't submit, I will."

Talking to Gyan left Sumi irritated. He was right, she had to find out the reason behind all this. She had known Mummyji to be nothing other than kind, loving and God-fearing. It did not make any sense. But who could she talk to? She knew she could count on Dev to listen to her, believe her and support her in whatever action she deemed fit. But he doted on Mummyji and this would break his heart. As far as Om bhaiyya was concerned, she had, so far, not had a single serious conversation with him and could not imagine doing so now. Mahima would blow her top at the mere suggestion and would sooner believe that Sumi had planted the bangle there herself than hear anything negative about Mummyji. Daddyji would listen. He would not like it, but he would know what was going on. He usually did. He would know what to do too. But she did not look forward to breaking this news to him either. What would happen if she approached Mummyji directly? What would she say? Would she explain and apologise or would she deny it?

Sumi went about the day with her mind going in circles. Unable to reach any conclusion, she distracted herself by thinking about her application. The deadline was less than a month away. After everyone had gone to bed, she brought her application to the dining table so that the light would not disturb Dev. The receipts were in her pencil case, where she was sure no one would care to look.

Mr Kapoor came to the kitchen to take his medicines. "Gyan should have stayed here for the night. He didn't even meet Dev and Om," he said.

Sumi waved her hand vehemently. "No, thank you. Three hours with him was quite enough to give me a headache."

Mr Kapoor laughed. "What did he say?"

Sumi realised that if there was ever a good time to talk to him, it was now.

"He is full of weird ideas. Says you cannot call a culprit a culprit until you know why they did what they did."

"That's a big line coming from such a young kid."

"You think so too?"

"Things are rarely straightforward."

"That's exactly what he says."

"This is not just any random philosophical debate that you are talking about, is it?"

Sumi lowered her eyes. She took out the receipts and pushed them towards him. He opened them gently and read.

"Where did you find them?" he asked, with not so much curiosity as trepidation.

Sumi kept quiet. Mr Kapoor pulled up a chair and sat down next to her.

"It's not what it looks like."

"You knew? Since when?"

"It's not like I knew. But one gets an inkling. For a few months. The gold in the locker was disappearing. That's our joint locker. No third person can open it."

"But why?

"*O my Mother, help me to my goal, O Rider of tigers, fill my empty bowl,*" he muttered softly.

"Om's blood pressure, his stress," he continued. "There is only one thing that can do that to Om: money. Markets crashed five months ago. By my calculations, he lost some principal too, although I am only working off estimates. But he doesn't want to sell that plot. He sees it as his only hope. So he is going to continue paying instalments on it. She is just trying to help him out."

Gyan's grinning face appeared before her eyes again and said, "Told you."

"What could I say?" Mr Kapoor said. "It is partly my fault. The one-and-half lakh for Vivek's college was a big drain on Om. I told him so many times that he need not pool in. Your mummy and I have fixed deposits. What are they for, if not for this? But once the decision was made, he sold off some shares in a hurry. He is the eldest, so he wants to act the eldest. He ended up selling some good ones. But at that time, I had to choose Vivek's future over Om's ambitions."

"I found it along with the missing bangle in her cupboard," Sumi said, for no particular reason.

"She has not had time to go to the jeweller with Vivek coming and Diwali and the wedding and all that."

Sumi looked at him.

"What do we do?"

"You are the most educated in this family. Do what you think is right, beta." He patted her shoulder and went to his room with tired steps.

Sumi had gone looking for a thief and had found something entirely else. An elder brother prematurely cashing his cleverly laid out investments to bail out his youngest brother, a mother contaminating a life's worth of good karma with petty thefts to save her eldest son's face, an all-seeing father turning a blind eye to the obvious, a young boy beating his already broken heart for letting his family down, a middle brother going about every day being a good elder brother, younger brother, son and husband. An entire family bending over backwards, some of them quietly, some not so quietly, some seen, others not, but all of them doing everything they could to hold on to each other.

And what about her? What had she done? She had found the culprit, but what was she going to do? Who would she tell about Mummyji? And what would she achieve by doing that? What "meaning" was she going to choose to superimpose on this?

The next time she found Daddyji alone, she gave him the receipts. "Can you please put them back in the coin purse under her saris for me?"

When no one is looking at the moon, it is not there.

The Elephant Sleeps

Sumi's application revisions had been nerve-racking. She had given up on hearing from her father, but Dev had sat with her, giving his input wherever he could, night after night, without losing patience or interest. After days of agonising over the length of her resume and her choice of words, Sumi finally decided that what they had was the best her application could get, so she went to the post office and mailed it to the university.

With the application out of the way, Sumi felt a void in her life. She found herself going through old copies of her application because that is what had consumed her mind for the last six months. It took her a few days to break the habit of looking for snatches of peaceful time to work on her application. She spent more time playing with Luv and Kush and apprenticing in the kitchen.

After days of cajoling, she finally managed to convince Mahima to do a recording with Hussain Sir, the multi-faceted music teacher from Sumi's school.

They left the house after tea and caught an auto to the radio station. Hussain Sir had arranged for an extra pair of headphones for Sumi to sit inside the recording room.

It was a small room. Two musicians sat on a mattress covered in a white bedsheet, one on the harmonium and the other on the tabla. They conferred for less than two minutes about the songs Mahima was going to sing, sounding out their scales and rhythms.

Sumi sat as far back as she could, so as not to disturb Mahima. She could still see her from the side. Mahima sang effortlessly, with her eyes closed, no crease on her forehead. She didn't even need to read the lyrics. She sang the two songs that she had prepared. Then she turned around and asked Hussain Sir if he had any requests and belted out two ghazals impromptu.

Once the recording was over, she turned back and looked at Sumi. Sumi made a circle with her thumb and forefinger and fanned the other three fingers to signal "super". Mahima nodded, concurring. Hussain Sir had a gentle smile on his lips. She had been blessed by Goddess Saraswati herself, he said. Would she consider doing a weekly programme, perhaps think of teaching? A rose's fragrance cannot be hidden for long, he added. Mahima soaked it all up with a controlled smile, like she was some celebrity artist, used to compliments.

Out in the reception, Om was waiting to take them home. Sumi introduced him to Hussain Sir, who greeted him and congratulated him for living with such an accomplished artist. Om had heard the live telecast and agreed vociferously with everything that Hussain Sir said. They thanked him for inviting Mahima and bade goodbye. In the car, Mahima sat next to Om in the front, and Sumi sat in the back. Mahima gave Om all the details of the recording room: how the tabla player was a young boy with no sense of rhythm, the harmonium player was drunk, the bedsheet had tea stains on it and the fan creaked.

Om interrupted her.

"And yet you sang like Lataji. I can't remember the last time I saw you this happy."

"Hussain Sir suggested I do a weekly programme."

"Today you look like the young girl whose hand I asked for in marriage six years ago."

"You mean I look old otherwise?"

Om attempted to remain poker-faced. Mahima turned back to look at Sumi and they both laughed.

"This is not fair," he complained. "I get it from both sides."

The whole neighbourhood had listened to her live programme and she became an instant celebrity in Shantinagar. When they reached home, Mahima recounted the experience to everyone all over again, and again the next day to Maya and Mrs Bansal, and again, for the next few days, to anyone who saw her.

Sumi heard from the Dean of the physics department within two weeks of posting the application. They sent a letter asking her to come for an interview the following week. She had never doubted that the interview call would come. It was a matter of when, not if – but even so, when it did arrive, she felt a twang of nervousness.

She told Dev that night, while he was helping her place

their ironed clothes in their cupboard. He was overjoyed. He stopped, turned to her and leaned forward in what, with any other person, would have been a hug. But he checked himself halfway and extended a hand in congratulations instead. They shook hands formally, awkwardly. Sumi would have much preferred the hug.

Dev had turned out to be a decent man. A man of his word and, lately, a good friend. He had stood by her solidly during the application process and she had no doubts that he would continue to do so during her PhD too. He had drawn a line to respect her ambitions and was guarding it with a zeal that was now beginning to bother Sumi. A few months ago, the line had given her comfort and reassurance. Now she worried that it had taken up roots deep in the ground between her and Dev, and was growing. What would happen if it grew into a wall? A wall so tall that neither of them could get over it, even if they wanted to. Like she did, now, at this moment. What if he did not?

He was saying he would take her there and drop her at school after the interview. He must have seen these worries scurrying over her face.

"What are you thinking?" he asked.

"Nothing."

"You don't look happy. This is such a big moment! This is what you wanted."

"Sometimes I wonder."

"Have you told Gyan?"

"Not yet. Why?"

"He needs to know. He wants this for you even more than you do."

Dev was right, of course. She knew this. She just had never acknowledged it. But she was surprised that Dev had sensed this. He had hardly spent any time with Gyan, yet he knew him as well as, maybe better than, she did. She went to bed irritated. What was the point of understanding electrons when you understood your own brother less than your husband did? When you could not say what exactly your husband felt for you? On the bed, the red elephant stared at her. Its eye was a careless knot of black thread that did not look happy. As Dev lay down on his side, the elephant rolled an inch closer to Sumi, squashed against her. It could barely breathe. Sumi was sure that it had grown larger since the last time she had seen it. It looked uncomfortable. There simply wasn't enough room on the bed anymore. Sumi sat up, held it in her lap and considered its face for a moment. There's a time and place for everything, she remembered from somewhere. She placed the bolster on the floor. She looked on to make sure the elephant was comfortable. It closed its eye. Was it sleeping or winking at her? Sumi sat back on the bed and turned to look at Dev. He was staring at the space vacated by the bolster. He looked up to meet Sumi's gaze. She saw her own reflection in his eyes. She saw sparks of love and desire sputtering under a constant drizzle of hesitation. Dev gulped. His Adam's apple bobbed. In this room heavy with shyness, it was the one thing that did not hold back, that called out to her, inviting her to touch it.

Rest Is Okay

The interview lasted over an hour. When Sumi came out, Dev could tell it had gone well. They got into the car and she told him all about it on their ride to school. The department had not seen an application as strong as hers in years. She had kept Professor Diwakar's name out of her application and the conversation, but he was a dazzling star in a small universe of physics, and once they found out that she grew up and studied in Allahabad, it did not take long for the panel to piece together who she was. They wanted to know about the papers she had published and the ones that she intended to write. They asked why she chose quantum physics and what practical usages she foresaw. Thanks to Gyan's incessant prodding, she was prepared and answered articulately. They said they would announce their decisions in a month, but their smiles told her she had made it. They sent their regards to her father.

At home that afternoon, everyone was eagerly waiting to know how it had gone. They sat her down and asked for the full account. She went over all the details all over again. When their curiosity was sated, Mrs Kapoor dialled Sumi's parents' number and handed the phone to her. Sumi recounted the interview one more time, to her mother.

"Well done," Lalita said. "It wasn't easy, doing this so soon after marriage."

It hadn't been. She had got sucked into life in Shantinagar with things that disappeared and reappeared, lights that went on and off, and hearts that broke and healed. If it had not been for Gyan's relentless, annoying nagging, she would have surely missed the deadline. Even now, he would tell her to hold her horses, it was just the interview, they were yet to admit her into the programme and, once again, he would be correct.

"It was just the interview," she said to her mother. "It's not like I've gotten through."

"For now, this is enough," Lalita said. "You had so many things going on, yet you managed everything well."

Sumi took this in. Lalita was the only one who had stood by her as she navigated her new home. She had been with her every step of the way, through letters, job connections, recipes, presents and phone calls.

"They send their regards to Baba. Is he there?" Sumi asked, although deep down she knew that she would not be able to speak to him today. Baba had left her to climb this mountain on her own and something told her that he would not be there to laud her as she neared the summit.

"He said he needed to go back to Haridwar for some more days. But he is well. I will write to him immediately and tell him about this. He will be very proud."

For as far back as she could remember, Sumi had considered herself and Baba as the A team, the intellectual camp, and Ma and Gyan the B team, the average camp. But when she had really needed support, Baba had disappeared without a word and it was her fence-sitting mother and irritating brother who had been there for her, making sure she didn't lose sight of her dreams, without expecting gratitude, knowing full well that she wouldn't appreciate or even acknowledge them. It was like they knew something she didn't.

"And you?" Sumi asked.

"I have always been proud of you, beta," Lalita said.

Mrs Kapoor took the phone from her and the mothers continued to talk. Maya and Mrs Bansal were coming over for tea. Sumi went to the kitchen. She put water to boil and set a tray with biscuits and snacks. She had recounted her interview details to so many people that it had begun to feel like something that had happened a long time ago, to someone else. Practically everyone had asked, except Baba.

She remembered a trip to Haridwar when she was twelve, all of them walking barefoot along the banks of the Ganga, watching devotees float bowls of leaves filled with flowers, coins and a lamp, that sailed away rocking gently on the cold water, shimmering against the setting sun. The soulful aarti sung by saffron-clad priests had the power to lure even the staunchest non-believer. She imagined Baba sitting on the steps, swaying to the aarti with his eyes closed. Did this concoction of gurgling water, pure air, music and incense give him the hope he was looking for? Would it last after the hymns were done? The next day, the bowls would wash up a few kilometres down the bank and begin to rot. The lamps, having lived their short lives, would be reduced to nothing more than lumps of clay and grease. Cows and dogs would nose through the leaves for food. Little boys would dive into the icy cold water to collect the coins. The divine beauty of the evening would morph into mortal ugliness in daylight. Which of these was the *real* reality? Sumi had no doubt that Baba was battling with his observations, arm-twisting the data to take a side. And until he did, he would not want to see her. Nor would he want her to see him.

She heard the ladies come in one by one and added milk, sugar, tea and cardamom to the saucepan.

She wished she could tell him not to worry. That it was all right to be in two states simultaneously. Although he knew it, far better than she did, he would not have allowed himself this superposition. She wanted to tell him that if electrons were doing it, maybe we could too, maybe we were supposed to, even. Maybe there was no one certain answer to reality. A single moment in space and time was a certainty, but when you took the space of a whole universe and placed it on a spectrum of endless time, what else did we expect to find other than a set of infinite possible realities? They would be pinned down to certainty when they would be pinned down. Until then, all we had was a probability curve of hope. Maybe that was what the electrons were trying to tell us, in their little, subatomic ways. If Baba was not able to hear it in the din of fear of his own mortality and the clanging of temple bells, she would help him hear it. She would write him a letter tonight. But before writing to the one who was questioning everything, she would write to Ma and Gyan, the two people who seemed to have held answers for her long before she had even figured out what her questions were.

She brought out the tea and sat with the ladies.

"Naina has convinced Nalini to accept BSc at Delhi University next year, if she doesn't get through medical this time," Maya was saying.

"Why? What's wrong with our City College?" Mahima asked.

"She will send Nalini next year, and she herself won't stay here a day longer than her twelfth exams. The three sisters will live together."

"What about the fees?" Mrs Bansal added.

"She doesn't want my money. She has enough saved, it seems. The three sisters can look after each other. 'You're free,' she said to me."

"What will you do alone?" Mahima asked.

"Whatever you say, Naina is one amazing girl. Has an eye for money," Mrs Bansal said.

"You know me. I'll be fine. I always am."

"What is it with our children? Vivek was also desperate to leave," Mahima said.

"I hardly got to see him this time," Maya complained.

"He left before he came. And he took the whole house

with him," Mahima said. "But this trip did him good. He looked happier when he left."

"It was good for us too," Mrs Bansal piped in. "I don't know what he said to Dhruv, but our son sprang a surprise on us last night. Says if he doesn't get through engineering this year, he will drop a year and try again next year. He said that he is beginning to understand some things when he sits down to study at night. Thank the Lord he is not planning on leaving us anytime soon."

"That's good," Maya said. "One boy has left, at least we get to see the other one around for some more time."

Sumi looked at Maya. They would never know why Maya did what she did, her reasons would forever remain a cloud of probabilities, impossible to pin down. What was she to make of her? Here was a woman who had single-handedly built a life for herself and her girls, who had been unafraid to stand up to the world to save her daughter from making a mistake. What did it feel like to live life like this, on your own terms? Sumi wondered. Was it liberating? Was loneliness the price she paid for it? Was her loneliness the reason she had flirted with the lights? Whatever Maya's reasons may have been, and however much chaos she had caused, it had ultimately brought Vivek and Nalini a little bit closer in the end and perhaps that was enough for now.

In the other corner of the room, the conversation between two mothers was coming to an end. Sumi heard Mrs Kapoor say, "Rest is okay," before she put the receiver down and joined the ladies on the sofa.

They did not say it facetiously. It was not a superior claim at normality, not after they had just bared their deepest worries to each other. Nor was it a mindless utterance. It was a wish and a hope. A reassurance to the other to not worry about all the troubles that they had just shared. The troubles were real, no doubt, and unrelenting. But so was life, and these difficulties were not going to cast too long a shadow on it as long as they kept talking to each other.

Daddyji had retreated at the prospect of being surrounded by these ladies. Sumi took two cups of tea and went up to his room.

Glossary

aarti	part of Hindu prayers in which light from a flame is waved to venerate deities while singing hymns, typically towards the end of a prayer
achar	a type of pickle in which the food is preserved in spiced oil
baraat	celebratory wedding procession that escorts the groom to the site of the wedding
besan	gram (chickpea) flour
beta	child
bhabhi	brother's wife; casually also used for brother-in-law's wife
bhaiyya	older brother
beedi	cheap cigarette made of unprocessed tobacco wrapped in leaves
bindi	decorative sticker worn on the centre of the forehead by women

Glossary

chakri	type of Diwali firecracker that goes on rotating on the ground, giving out light
Chitrahaar	programme broadcast on the national channel Doordarshan in the 1980s and 1990s, featuring songs from Hindi films
darshan	literally "glimpse" or "view"; mainly used in context of the auspicious sight of a deity or a holy person
daseri	variety of Indian mango known for its sweetness and fragrance
dharamshala	public resthouse or shelter, often charitable
didi	older sister
elaichi	cardamom
filmi	colloquial term meaning "dramatic", like in films
gangajal	water from the river Ganges, considered holy
gayatri mantra	a sacred mantra from the *Rig Veda*, an ancient Hindu canonical text
gudiya	doll
"Hain?"	expression of surprise or confusion, similar to "Sorry, what?" or "Beg your pardon?"
Hanuman Chalisa	a devotional hymn in praise of Lord Hanuman

Glossary

kadhai gosht	meat (gosht) slow-cooked in a traditional round-bottomed pot (kadhai)
kaleere	bridal jewellery; dangling ornaments worn on the wrists
khus	vetiver, a type of grass traditionally used as a coolant
kulhad	clay cup typically used by small tea vendors
langda	variety of Indian mango known for its distinctive scent, nuanced flavour and generous amount of flesh
loo	a strong, dusty, gusty, hot and dry summer wind
Mahabharat	one of the two major Sanskrit epics of ancient India revered in Hinduism
mata ki chowki	a spiritual gathering for the Mother Goddess involving prayers and hymns
mathri	fried, savoury, flaky biscuit
pallu	the loose end of a sari, worn over one shoulder or the head
papdi chaat	crispy fried-dough wafers served with typical chaat ingredients such as chickpeas, boiled potatoes, yogurt sauce, and tamarind and coriander chutneys

Glossary

pheras	ritual in Hindu, Sikh, and other Indic wedding ceremonies where the couple walks around a sacred fire or object
pitthoo	porter
prasad	devotional offering made to a god, typically consisting of a sweet that is later shared amongst devotees
qabristaan	cemetery or graveyard
rajma chawal	kidney beans and rice
shehnai	South Asian reed instrument that is often played at weddings and other ceremonies
tikka	piece of jewellery placed in between the middle hair parting, usually with a pendant that drops down to the forehead

Acknowledgements

It takes a village to create a book. My foremost thanks to Unbound Firsts for creating a space for writers of colour to tell their stories. Thank you Aliya for championing this book and believing that this story deserves to be told.

Thank you Flo for patiently editing through the many, many rounds, helping me polish this book to its best version.

I am grateful to Shelley Weiner, my instructor at Faber, for all the sage writing advice and to my fabulous Faber cohort for the workshops and discussions, chapter after chapter. Extra special thanks to Matilda for all those mornings at the British Library when we kept showing up and putting in the work.

Thank you Rivka for keeping me sane and to my Ochre Sky writing circle for holding me through the highs and lows of the publishing journey.

Thank you Shireesh for reading the (way too) early drafts and giving feedback while not letting the marriage fall apart. To Sifat, the most ruthless ten-year-old editor there ever shall be and to Rish, for his gentle honesty in not giving this book the time of day.

Acknowledgements

Lastly, my deepest gratitude to my parents, my grandma and my brother for a childhood that was a kaleidoscope of family ties and friendships – the inspiration for this book.

unbound FIRSTS

Our Unbound Firsts books are inspired by Unbound's mission to discover new voices, fresh talent and amazing stories. We're proud to offer emerging writers of colour the opportunity to be published by an award-winning publishing house and have their stories shared with readers around the world.

There's an Unbound Firsts book for every reader – whether it's a gripping mystery set in underground Moscow, a time-travelling historical fantasy, or a bold multi-generational debut exploring themes of queerness, revolution and Islamic sisterhood.

Perhaps you're after an uplifting read about following your heart against all odds or are yearning to be transported to Tokyo during cherry blossom season. A contemporary family saga which cleverly blends the laws of quantum physics with everyday suburban life completes the collection.

Unbound Firsts is a celebration of new writing for readers everywhere. Discover the full collection and dive into your next read today.

(**Unbound Firsts** 🔍)

A Note on the Type

Sabon is an old-style serif typeface designed in the mid-sixties by German-born typographer and designer Jan Tschichold (1902–1974). It is a classic typeface for body text, popular in book design.

Tschichold was commissioned by Walter Cunz at Stempel to design a new typeface, as requested by the German Master Printers Association, that could be printed identically on Linotype, Monotype or letterpress machines. The intention being to simplify the process of planning lines and pagination when printing a book.

The design of the roman is based on the classical types of Claude Garamond.